ANIMAL PASSIONS

Busy vet Jane Pardoe is happy. She's living the dream of running her own practice. The only cloud on the horizon is the relationship between her young son Callum and his father. Jane wonders if they should reconcile and be a proper family again. But there are complications: Jane can't deny the attraction between herself and Liam Delahaye, in charge of the horses at the Ashington Estate. But is he really the right man for her?

GEORGIE FOORD

ANIMAL
PASSIONS

Complete and Unabridged

LINFORD
Leicester

First published in Great Britain in 2011

First Linford Edition
published 2012

British Library CIP Data

Foord, Georgie.
  Animal passions. - -
  (Linford romance library)
  1. Love stories.
  2. Large type books.
  I. Title II. Series
  823.9'2–dc23

  ISBN 978–1–4448–1108–7

Published by
F. A. Thorpe (Publishing)
Anstey, Leicestershire

Set by Words & Graphics Ltd.
Anstey, Leicestershire
Printed and bound in Great Britain by
T. J. International Ltd., Padstow, Cornwall

This book is printed on acid-free paper

1

The two men — one tall, slim, in his early thirties, the other shorter, elderly — leaned side by side on the stable door. They watched the handsome chestnut stallion pacing restlessly, pawing with iron-shod hooves at the straw covering the cobbled floor. He rolled his eyes at the men, tossing his head and from time to time lifting his foreleg as if in some discomfort.

'Well, what do you think, Delahaye?' The older man spoke first. 'Doesn't look too bad to me. I really need him to be ready for tomorrow. Not worth calling the vet out, surely?'

The younger man thought for a moment before replying.

'Sultan's your horse, Lord Ashby. I don't think there's much to worry about, but in my opinion it's better to be safe than sorry. You don't want to risk putting the horse out of action for weeks. I really think we should get the vet to come and take a look.'

The aristocratic ex-soldier puffed out his cheeks and pulled at his greying military-style moustache. He didn't want to take the younger man's advice, but he had learned enough about his new stud manager already to know that he would not easily be put off.

'Oh very well. Do it, if you think it best.'

The horse put his head over the stable door and nudged the old man. George Ashby, the eighth Earl of Ashington, patted the silky-smooth neck.

'Good boy, Sultan,' he murmured affectionately. 'Soon have you back out on the gallops.'

★　★　★

Jane stripped off her disposable gloves and dropped them in the bin. Pushing her unruly auburn hair back behind her ears, she plonked herself on the stool at the counter, resting her head on her elbows. She was exhausted.

'That's the last one, Jane.' Vicky bustled back into the surgery, trim in her nurse's green scrubs. 'Hectic this evening, or what? Sod's law, isn't it — quiet all week, then all hell let loose on a Friday. That's definitely the busiest we've been for ages.'

Jane looked up wearily. 'Hectic? Verging on chaotic. It was those two moggies having a go at each other in the waiting room that almost finished me off. I was within an ace of banning the both of them — only we need their custom. I don't know which were worse — the cats or their owners!'

She hauled herself back to her feet. 'You get off home now, Vicky. You've done more than enough today. You don't want to keep your red-hot date waiting, do you? I'll clean up here and with a bit of luck I'll be home to spend some time with Callum before his bedtime.'

The young nurse smiled sympathetically. She knew how hard her boss worked. It wasn't easy being a single mum, and holding down a demanding career like that of a veterinary surgeon.

'That's okay, Jane. Jason can wait. The two of us will get it done in half the time. You do the floor in here, and I'll see to the waiting room. I'm sure there must be a puppy puddle somewhere!'

She's a good girl, Jane thought. She was fond of Vicky. She was young, but bright as a button and keen to learn, well on the way to becoming a first-rate nurse. She was good with the animals — and their owners, which was sometimes a lot more tricky. She had a calm and confident way with them which made Jane's job a whole lot easier.

Jane looked around the small surgery, with its stainless steel examination table and instruments in the steriliser, the most up-to-date equipment she could afford. She sighed. One day, perhaps, if she could build the practice up, she might be able to afford the luxury of some help. Vicky was great as practice nurse and receptionist, but that was as far as her expertise went.

Jane loved her job. Even as a small child, when she'd been given her first hamster, she'd wanted to be a vet. When old Mr Johnson retired eight months ago, she'd jumped at the opportunity to take over his practice.

But the future was not entirely rosy. Jane had found problems with the accounts almost immediately. Mr Johnson had been too soft; some of his elderly clients had not been billed at all. All very nice and cosy, but the drugs bills needed paying — and now that Jane was having to ask those same clients to pay their way, her popularity was dwindling.

To add to her woes, the wealthy clients, the farms and estates, had defected to the upmarket Riverside practice, with its team of specialist vets, shiny new clinics and state-of-the-art operating theatres. She'd have to find some source of new income soon, or her dream of running her own business could come to a premature end.

She wondered if she should ask Steve for his advice. He was the money expert, but he'd been dismissive of her ambition to run her own business. He had warned her that she'd have problems; the last thing she wanted to do was to admit that he was right.

Vicky popped her head round the door. 'All clean and tidy in there, Jane. I'll be off now, if that's okay?' She paused. 'And don't forget my birthday drink at the Ash tomorrow night, will you?'

Jane smiled. 'As if I could forget. You've been dropping enough hints all week! Off you go, and don't do anything I wouldn't do.' They shared a smile.

Jane heard the outside door bang shut. Flopping into a chair, she pulled out her mobile and selected 'home' in her address book.

'Mum? Sorry I'm so late. We've had

quite a time of it this evening. I'll tell you about it when I get home. Can you get Callum ready for bed? I'll read him a story before he goes to sleep.'

Jane didn't know what she'd do without her mother. Steve had abandoned her with a small baby, and she'd been only too grateful when Cathy had announced she was moving in. It had worked brilliantly. Cathy was a mum in a million, Jane thought gratefully. Always there when she was wanted, ready to help — but never once had she said, 'I told you so.'

Jane had been nineteen when she met Steve. She'd fallen head over heels for his blond good looks and smooth charm. Even now, eight years on, the thought of his hands running over her back brought a shiver of desire.

They'd married much too soon — she'd only just graduated — but she was so much in love that nothing anyone could say, least of all her concerned mother, could make her change her mind.

Then, just as she'd started her first job, she'd found she was pregnant.

At first Steve had been as pleased about the baby as she was, despite the bad timing, and for a while after Callum was born he'd been a loving father. Then, when Callum was just six months old, he'd simply walked out.

They'd survived, somehow, with the help and support of her mother. But Jane was torn apart with grief and loneliness.

Now Callum was coming up for seven years old, she'd got her own business and her life was back on track. The one thing she didn't want, or need, was another man in her life.

The telephone interrupted her thoughts. It was almost half-past seven on a Friday evening. *It had better be a real emergency*, she thought.

'Hello? Jane Pardoe, Maybury Pet-Care here. Can I help?'

'Miss Pardoe, this is Liam Delahaye. I'm calling from Lord Ashby's estate. I'd like you to come right away and have a look at one of our horses.'

'But Lord Ashby is one of Riverside's clients,' Jane protested.

The deep, arrogant voice, with an intriguing lilt of — what? Jane couldn't quite place it: Welsh? Scottish? — overruled her.

'They have no one available, and this is an emergency. Come at once, if you please.'

Jane thought swiftly. She was longing to get home. It had been such a busy day, and all she wanted was to curl up with Callum on the sofa, with his story books, and a glass of wine. But Lord Ashby was an important client, and if she could get some of the estate work, it would do wonders for her credibility with the other big landowners and farmers in the county. Not to mention her bank balance!

'Very well, Mr Delahaye. I'll be with you as soon as I can.'

Sighing, Jane phoned her mother again. 'Really sorry, Mum, I've just received an emergency callout. Kiss

Callum goodnight for me, and tell him I'll see him in the morning.'

Checking the contents of her medical bag, Jane took a last look round the sparkling-clean surgery and snapped off the lights.

* * *

In the darkened stableyard, Liam Delahaye paced restlessly, constantly looking at his watch. He shivered in the chill evening breeze and thought longingly of his cosy cottage with its tiny garden, awash now with daffodils, with the promise of old-fashioned roses and lavender to come. He pictured the logs glowing in the wood burner, and could almost smell the aroma of the casserole slow-cooking in the oven. Fenella had been furious when he told her he had to go out, but a summons from Lord Ashby could not be ignored. He pictured her curled on his sofa, loose-limbed and sleek as an exotic cat. The thought almost made him abandon his vigil in the stableyard.

He checked his watch for the twentieth time. 'Come on, woman,' he muttered. 'What's keeping you?' He hunched his chin into his collar and thrust his hands deep into his pockets, seething with impatience.

Jane drove as fast as she dared through the twisting, narrow lanes. She concentrated on the road ahead, aware that it would be almost impossible to spot a fox or badger in the darkness.

She'd driven past the entrance to the estate many times, but had never ventured inside the grounds. Lord Ashby was known as a difficult man who liked his privacy. Jane hoped she wouldn't have to meet him. She remembered seeing a report in the local paper some weeks ago about the new stud manager at the estate. There'd been a fuzzy photo of a tall, lean man shaking Lord Ashby's hand, and Jane had been struck by the younger man's arrogant pose and confident demeanour. She had an uncomfortable feeling that Liam Delahaye was going to be a force to be reckoned with.

The car headlights picked out the two great pillars at the entrance gates. She followed the driveway into the stable yard, in darkness apart from a single lit loose box at the far end. The tall, slim figure of a man stood in the beam of light.

'The great Mr Delahaye, I presume,' Jane muttered to herself.

The movement of the car activated the security lights and in an instant the yard was bathed in harsh, white light.

Liam waved the car over and strode to meet it. Jane climbed out of the driving seat and held out her hand. 'Jane Pardoe,' she said.

Delahaye ignored her polite gesture. 'About time, too. I don't want to be here all night. The horse is over here.'

Jane was left gaping at the man's rudeness. *A bit of common courtesy wouldn't go amiss*, she thought crossly, trailing in his wake across the yard.

The big chestnut horse was magnificent. He moved restlessly in his stable, disturbed by the presence of a stranger, stamping his hooves and tossing his mane. To Jane, he looked a virtually perfect specimen. She hadn't been pleased to get the callout, but had to admit that it was a privilege to be asked to treat such a beautiful animal.

'So what's the problem?'

Liam looked at her as if she was an idiot.

'Isn't it obvious? The horse is lame. Lord Ashby is hoping he will be fit to ride tomorrow.'

Jane bit her tongue. To her, the horse looked in wonderful condition — no trace of lameness and not needing an emergency callout.

She moved to enter the box. 'I'd better come in with you,' said Liam. 'Sultan can be a bit unpredictable.'

He held the horse's head while Jane crouched at his feet and ran her hands down Sultan's slender legs. She was uncomfortably aware of the lean, powerful man standing close behind her, watching her every move. He'd been curt to the point of rudeness, yet now his strong, capable hands stroked the horse's neck, calming the restless animal with gentle movements, soothing its fear. Forcing herself to concentrate, she found a tiny swelling on the horse's foreleg, which to her eyes did not seem serious, but in the circumstances she decided to play it safe.

'There's a small heat spot here, which should clear up in a couple of days if the horse is rested. I don't think it would be wise for Lord Ashby to ride him out for a few days. Sorry if that causes you a problem.'

Liam pursed his lips and frowned.

'That's not what his lordship will want to hear. I'd better call him.' He reached in his pocket for his mobile. 'Lord Ashby, the vet's here. No, not from Riverside. A young woman from the small town practice. Cats, dogs, budgies — that sort of thing. Mmm, she seems competent enough, but . . . '

Jane couldn't believe what she was hearing. The arrogance of the man! With an effort she kept the lid on her temper.

Delahaye handed the phone to her. 'He wants a word with you.'

'Hello? Jane Pardoe here.'

The voice in her ear was commanding and expected to be obeyed.

'Now look here, one my guests is keen to ride that horse tomorrow and I want you to pass him A-one. He had a small knock yesterday but in my opinion he's perfectly fit. I don't believe in mollycoddling horses — nor men for that matter, what?'

What? thought Jane, then realised it was just the retired officer's military manner of speaking.

'Lord Ashby, I am a qualified, professional veterinary surgeon, well able to treat horses as well as dogs and budgies. The horse has a small sprain. I would recommend that he be rested for a few days and not taken out. That's my professional opinion; if you choose to ignore it, that's up to you.'

There was silence at the other end of the phone. Jane glanced at Liam, wondering if she'd said too much. To her surprise there was a gleam of something approaching amusement in the dark eyes.

'Lord Ashby,' she continued, 'I apologise if I've appeared rude. It's just that, as a vet, I would hate to see this beautiful horse seriously injured.'

Lord Ashby harrumphed in her ear and blustered in his upper-crust voice. 'You're a very outspoken young woman. But you probably know what you're talking about. I'll consider what you have said. Good evening.'

The call was abruptly terminated and Jane silently handed the phone back to Liam. *That's torn it,* she thought miserably. *No hope of any more estate work now. I'll be blacklisted for sure.*

Liam Delahaye walked her back to her car. 'Send me your bill,' he said briefly. 'I'll be in touch if the horse doesn't improve.'

Some thanks would be nice, Jane thought, reaching for the seat belt.

'Oh, and by the way, nobody speaks to Lord Ashby like that.'

Jane glanced up at him. The harsh light slanted off his hair, black as a raven's wing, and sculpted his saturnine face into sharply angled planes. A sweep of dark stubble shadowed the jutting jawline. To her surprise, a trace of a smile hovered round the finely chiselled lips.

He nodded to her. 'That was well done,' he said. 'Lord Ashby won't like it, but if it's any consolation, I agree with you.'

Unbidden, the answer to her earlier query came to her. Irish — that was the intriguing lilt in his voice. Liam Delahaye was Irish.

Jane drove home, more slowly this time, trying to make sense of what had just happened. Had she really laid down the law to a member of the aristocracy? And what did Liam Delahaye make of her? she wondered. In spite of herself she felt a shiver of excitement, adrenalin still running though her veins. *It would be interesting to get to know him better,* she thought. Maybe their paths would cross again. She rather hoped they would.

Alone in the stable yard, Liam watched the car lights disappear out of the gates, and the sound of the engine grew fainter as Jane drove away down the lane. He stood for a moment, reliving their encounter. *A difficult young woman,* he thought. *Self-opinionated and a bit too sure of herself.*

He liked his women tall, slim and blonde, not small and outspoken — and certainly not auburn, with, he suspected, a rare temper to go with the hair. That hair! Almost the same colour as the horse, he'd thought, watching her in the stable as she worked. But she'd handled Sultan well and had cared enough about him to stand up to Lord Ashby.

Liam had been aware for some time that the newly-established Riverside vets were beginning to take the Estate's custom for granted. Jane Pardoe, he thought, might be worth getting to know a little better. He turned on his heel and made his way back to his cottage, his supper, and his woman.

2

'Morning, Mum.' Jane, yawning widely, leaned her elbows on the kitchen worktop. 'Sorry I was so late last night, and thanks again for looking after Callum for me.'

Cathy bustled round the kitchen in her efficient, businesslike way. 'You look wrecked, love. Here, get this down you.' She pushed a mug of tea across the counter to her daughter.

Callum, in his Batman pyjamas, was kneeling on a chair at the kitchen table finishing his boiled egg and soldiers. He gave his mother a reproachful look. 'You never came and said goodnight like you promised, Mummy. I stayed awake for ages, but you forgot.'

Jane felt a pang of guilt. She knelt down beside her son and hugged him.

'I am sorry, darling. I didn't forget. I did try very hard to be home in time, but I had to go and look at a poorly horse.'

The little boy squirmed in her embrace, not quite ready to forgive.

'Tell you what,' continued Jane coaxingly, 'we'll have two stories tonight and you can have some of my special bubbles in your bath. Okay?'

Callum considered for a moment, deciding it was a good enough bargain. 'Okay,' he said cheerfully, sliding down from his chair and disappearing in the direction of his playroom. Honey, the family's Labrador, opened one eye, then heaved herself out of her basket and padded after Callum. The small boy's self-appointed guardian.

Jane yawned again and slumped in her chair, pushing her hands though her tousled hair. Cathy tut-tutted. 'Come on, love. Wakey-wakey. Steve's coming for Callum at ten, remember.'

Jane clasped her hands round the mug, which bore the legend *I Love Dogs*, and took a sip. She'd lain awake for hours after she finally got to bed, and then had weird dreams about running along a beach, chased by a pantomime-type squire on a huge black horse, cracking a whip. She'd woken exhausted and her eyes felt gritty, her limbs heavy.

'So how was the great Lord Ashby's estate?' asked Cathy. 'Too posh for the likes of us, I don't doubt.'

'I only saw the stable yard, Mum. I was nowhere near the house. The horse was gorgeous, and nothing much wrong with it. But I did speak to Lord Ashby.' Jane smiled at the memory. 'In fact, I think I was a bit bossy.'

'Oh, love, I hope you weren't rude. I know you! You're too hasty for your own good sometimes. You don't want to get on the wrong side of His Lordship. You need to let them know what a good vet you are.'

'It's okay, Mum, really. The manager, Mr Delahaye, he backed me up — well, sort of.' She jumped up from the table. She didn't want to think about Liam.

'I'll go and have a quick shower, then get Callum ready for his dad.'

* * *

Steve was late, as usual. Callum was standing on the sofa by the window in the front room, bouncing with frustration as cars came up the road and failed to stop. At last he recognised his dad's expensive motor gliding to a halt outside the gate, and dashed to the front door to greet his part-time parent.

Jane thought, not for the first time, that it was easy to be a popular dad when you only saw your child every other week. And Steve now had the spare money to lavish on the boy.

It had been different when Callum was a baby and they'd lived in a small flat. He couldn't wait to get away then, she remembered. But now that Callum was a bright, talkative and endearing little boy, things were different. Now he was happy to take the child out, to

23

introduce him to his friends as 'my son'. He lavished money on Callum, in spite of Jane asking him not to, buying expensive treats, making Jane feel shabby and second-best.

Cathy reassured her. 'Callum knows who loves him best,' she soothed whenever Jane felt down. 'You can't buy your way into a child's heart.'

But Jane couldn't help a nagging feeling that Callum was missing out, living with herself and his grandmother. Boys needed a strong, masculine presence, didn't they? Callum needed his father around more often than every other weekend.

Jane opened the door to Steve. Callum threw himself at his father and grabbed him round the knees, almost knocking him over. 'Dad! Dad! I've been waiting forever. I thought you'd forgotten to come.'

Steve picked his son up, hugging him. 'Forget you, my lad? Never!'

Jane gritted her teeth, willing herself to keep quiet. She stared at the two of them, so alike with their fair hair and blue eyes.

'Callum, go and fetch your jacket,' she said. 'Daddy's waiting to go.' She looked at Steve. 'Where are you taking him today?' she asked. 'Please don't stuff him too full of junk food, will you? It's not good for him.'

Steve laughed. 'You fuss too much. He can't eat rabbit food all his life.'

'Steve,' Jane began, then hesitated, not sure how to go on. 'I was wondering — maybe we could spend some time together sometime? You, me and Callum, as a family?'

Steve frowned. 'Hmmm, I don't know, Jane — maybe that wouldn't be such a good idea. I'll have to think about it.'

Jane felt as though she'd been slapped in the face. She hadn't expected to be dealt quite such a blatant put-down. Humiliated, she turned away and pretended to fiddle with the flowers on the hall table.

Callum reappeared, zipped up and

ready to go. Jane bent to kiss him, hiding her feelings. 'Bye, sweetie, have a lovely time. Be good for Daddy.'

She felt a huge pang of regret for what might have been; the waste of a promising marriage. She allowed herself, just for a moment, to imagine what it would be like to be a whole family unit — Steve, Callum and herself. It might be possible, even now, she thought, to patch things up, try again — even if Steve had made it clear he wasn't keen on the idea right now.

Surely it would be worth one last throw of the dice. She'd have to try and convince him of how good it would be for their beloved Callum to have his mum and dad back together.

Unbidden, an image of Liam Delahaye popped into her mind. Where on earth did he come from? She shook her head, trying to clear her thoughts.

I need some fresh air, she told herself. *I'm not thinking straight*.

'Mum,' she called. 'I'm taking Honey for some exercise.'

Jane loaded the dog into the car, and headed out of town to the wide open spaces of the common, where she could let her off the lead for a good run. Honey was a well-trained, obedient animal and Jane was confident about letting her go. The big yellow dog bounded away, nose down, following some irresistible scent.

The fresh air and brisk wind whipped colour into Jane's cheeks as she jogged over the short, springy turf. The line of trees away to her left, hazy with the first pale green leaves of spring, marked the boundary, Jane realised, of the Ashington Estate. She paused, catching her breath, and unwelcome thoughts of the previous evening's events filled her mind.

What is going on? she thought. *I was just doing my job, after all.* She treated dozens of animals every week. Lord Ashby's horse was no longer her concern. And she was unlikely ever to cross paths with Liam Delahaye again.

Honey's urgent barking drew Jane's

mind back to the here-and-now. To her horror she saw a big chestnut thoroughbred, galloping out of control, its rider clinging on for dear life, heading her way out of the woodland. Jane instantly recognised Sultan, and for a moment she froze, wondering what to do. Then anger flared. 'He ignored my advice!' she muttered. 'Stupid old man — why get me all that way out there if he wasn't going to take any notice of what I said?'

A moment later she saw a Land Rover bumping over the turf towards her. The driver waved urgently to her and shouted, 'If I head him off, can you try and grab the reins?' With a jolt, Jane realised it was Liam Delahaye.

Gradually he managed to manoeuvre the vehicle into a circle around the horse, slowing its frantic pace until, exhausted and sweating, Sultan came to a halt, head down, flanks heaving.

Jane approached cautiously, hand outstretched; speaking in a low, calm voice. 'Steady, lad. Whoa there, good boy, Sultan. Easy now.' The horse allowed her to take hold of the reins. She smoothed its silky neck, damp under her fingers, and felt the animal relax, its panic subsiding.

The young rider slid out of the saddle and collapsed in an undignified heap on the grass. He sat for a moment, winded, then staggered to his feet, dusting himself down. He looked, Jane thought, very embarrassed.

'Delahaye!' he called to Liam. 'Can you come and give me a hand?'

Liam was running across to Jane, ignoring the rider, his attention all for the horse. 'I'll take over now.' He grabbed the reins. 'God knows what that fool of a boy has done,' he muttered, then raised his voice. 'Quickly! Check that leg for damage, will you?'

Jane looked at him with undisguised dislike, unable to believe the man's rudeness. 'Good morning, Mr Delahaye,' she said icily. 'Am I to understand you wish to call upon my veterinary services again?'

The man stared at her, his flinty eyes cold and mocking.

'I beg your pardon, Miss Pardoe,' he said with exaggerated courtesy. 'Would you be so kind as to take a look at the horse while I assist the rider into the Land Rover?'

Jane ran her hands over the horse, checking its legs, feeling for further damage. She straightened up, dusting off her hands on the seat of her jog pants. 'The good news is that I can find no more damage. But that's down to luck. The horse could easily have been seriously hurt.'

Liam breathed a huge sigh of relief and relaxed, leaning against the bonnet of the car. His well-worn jeans hugged the contours of his body, outlining long legs and muscular thighs. Jane's eyes travelled up past the flat stomach, slim waist and broad torso to the open neck of a checked shirt revealing a suntanned throat. The angles of his face looked softer and less forbidding in sunlight. He looked different, somehow, Jane thought; more approachable. He really did care about the horse, she realised. Maybe it was anxiety that made him so aggressive and unpleasant.

Careful, she warned herself. *You'll be liking the man if you don't watch it.*

The horse, calm now, bent its head to crop the short, succulent turf. Liam patted the sleek chestnut neck with a gentle, competent hand. A strong, square hand, Jane noted, continuing her personal inventory, with short, well-kept nails. His shirt sleeves were rolled up to the elbow, revealing the strong sun-browned forearms of a man who lived his life outdoors.

'I take it Lord Ashby ignored my advice?' she said, trying not to sound accusing. Liam gave a short bark of a laugh.

'Hah! it wasn't his Lordship's fault. Lord Ashby gave instructions that the horse was to be rested, but his nephew ignored him and took the horse out without telling anyone. Lord Ashby told him Sultan was injured, and that anyway the horse would be too much of a handful for him. But the talk in the stableyard is that Edmund Faraday is accustomed to getting his own way.'

'Edmund . . . ?'

'Yes, Mr Edmund Faraday. Even though he doesn't have a title, he's Lord Ashby's heir. His sister's only son. Lord Ashby has a daughter, but no son and heir to carry on the dynasty.'

Jane thought Liam knew rather a lot about the family. After all, he was only a member of staff, wasn't he?

A cloud crossed Liam's face. He frowned. 'I wonder what happened to spook the horse?'

Honey trotted up to Jane and pushed her nose against her knee. Jane bent to scratch the dog between her ears, careful to keep herself between the dog and the horse.

'Hey! Something put up a pheasant in the woods. That's what made the horse bolt. I bet it was that dog!' Edmund Faraday was leaning out of the car window pointing at Honey. 'I might have been killed. That damned dog shouldn't be allowed to run around on its own.'

'Now wait a minute.' Jane's temper was always close to the surface where her child or her dog was concerned. 'This is my dog and there's no way she scared your horse. She was on the common, within my sight, all the time and I know she never went near the wood.'

'And who are you, young woman?'

Liam stepped forward. 'This is Miss Pardoe, the vet who advised Sultan should be rested.' Edmund had the grace to look embarrassed. Liam went on, 'I don't believe her dog is to blame, sir, I think you're mistaken.'

'Well, we'll see what my uncle has to say about this. Lucky for you I wasn't badly hurt.' Edmund retreated back inside the car, sulking.

Liam turned to Jane. 'I'm so sorry, after all you've done. I'll see that Lord Ashby has the full facts, I promise.' He smiled at her, a full, genuine smile that lit up his face. With her red-gold hair tied up — more fox's brush than ponytail — her fair complexion innocent of make-up and with a shower of freckles across her nose, she looked like a child, he thought. His dark eyes warmed as his gaze travelled the length of her body and back to her jade-green eyes, and Jane felt herself blush under his scrutiny. She felt an unexpected lurch in the pit of her stomach.

Hey, what's going on here? she reprimanded herself. A shiver ran down her spine in spite of the warmth of the spring sunshine.

'Is there anything more I can do?' she asked. 'How are you going to get Sultan home?'

Liam frowned, considering the question. 'I could ring the yard and ask them to bring the horsebox. Or do you think it would be safe for me to walk him — slowly, of course?'

'You won't do any more damage if you take it gently,' Jane decided, adding to herself that she could always make another visit to the stables if necessary. Liam smiled again and nodded, glancing across at the Land Rover. 'The young Squire can drive himself back. I'll be careful with Sultan, don't you worry.' He bent over to run his hands down the horse's legs, picking its feet up to check for stones. He stood at the horse's shoulder, smoothing the satiny chestnut neck, a man in command of his environment.

The wind ruffled his black hair and he ran a hand through it in a boyish gesture, pushing a lock away from his eyes. He paused for a moment, thoughtful, looking down at Jane. 'Well, goodbye then. I hope I'll not need to trouble you again.' He took the reins in his right hand, spoke softly to the horse and moved away towards the woodland path, not looking back.

Jane watched him go in a turmoil of emotion. She had forgotten about Edmund Faraday. Turning, she found him standing behind her, apparently recovered from his shock. A tall, gangling young man, barely out of his teens. She felt a pang of something approaching sympathy for him. He'd been caught out, taken the horse when he shouldn't, and then been unable to control it. Thankfully he'd suffered no injury, other than to his pride. And now he was trying to pin the blame on Honey.

He smiled at Jane, trying to ingratiate himself. 'Now, young woman, about that Labrador bitch of yours.' Jane took a step back, realising she was alone. Edmund put his hand on her arm. 'I might be prepared to forget all about it. You look like a nice sensible girl. No need for any trouble with the law. I'm sure we can come to some arrangement, between ourselves.'

Jane was surprised to find herself feeling almost amused. This boy, propositioning her? She pretended to be outraged.

'How dare you!' she said icily. 'My dog did nothing wrong. If you couldn't control the horse, don't try and blame anyone else.'

As he took a step closer, Honey

pushed herself in front of him and growled softly, deep in her throat. Jane stared at him, determined to outface him, then turned and walked back towards her car with Honey by her side, leaving Edmund red-faced with frustration at being out-manoeuvred.

'You've not heard the last of this!' he' shouted after her. 'My solicitor will be getting in touch, I promise you.'

★　★　★

The Ashby Arms, known to its regulars as 'the Ash', was a quintessential English country pub, much loved by locals and tourists alike. It was always busy on Saturday nights, and Jane was lucky to find a space in the car park. On this warm, spring evening the bar door stood open. A handful of beer drinkers were standing outside with their pints and cigarettes, chatting easily as old friends do, with an occasional burst of laughter. A blackboard outside advertised a forthcoming visit by a folk group.

Jane sat in her car, not really in the mood to join Vicky's birthday celebration. She was trying to make sense of Steve's coldness towards her that morning. Why, she wondered, would he be so reluctant to spend time with her? Callum had come home happy and chattering about his day out — the visit to the funfair down on the seafront, fish and chips for lunch and a kickabout with his football on the blowy, windswept beach. *A proper lads' day out*, thought Jane, *no hint of any female company*.

But the question she'd heard her son ask Cathy when she was giving him his tea would haunt her for days.

'Grandma,' he'd said, 'why does Dad have to live in a different house?'

Cathy had sidestepped the awkward moment, distracting the boy with a question about what flavour of milkshake he preferred.

What is wrong with me? Jane asked herself. She was still the same girl Steve had fallen in love with — how many years ago was it? Eight? Nine, maybe. She'd been a student then. Perhaps she'd grown too career-minded for him. With a sigh, she made an effort to tear herself away from her troubles. Tonight belonged to Vicky and there was no way Jane was going to spoil it for her by being a party pooper.

She wove her way past the al fresco drinkers and into the gloom of the crowded saloon bar. 'Jane! Over here!' Vicky, surrounded by her friends, was waving at her from the corner, where a flotilla of fluorescent pink helium balloons dancing over the table announced that she was the Birthday Girl.

Jane hugged her young assistant, glad of her uncomplicated friendship after the turmoil and mixed emotions of the last twenty-four hours. She pushed her carefully wrapped parcel and card across the table. 'Here you are, old lady. Happy birthday — what is it, twenty-two now? You'll be collecting your bus pass next!'

Vicky giggled, flushed with excitement, blonde hair fluffed out round her pretty face. Jane was used to seeing her in green scrubs with her hair tucked away under a cap. 'Hey!' she exclaimed. 'How did you get so gorgeous all of a sudden? Where's Jason? I hope he appreciates you!'

'He certainly does.' Jane turned to see Vicky's partner making his way back from the bar, his hands full of brimming glasses. 'I got a Chardonnay for you, Jane, hope that's okay?'

'Perfect!' Jane took the frosty glass from him carefully and raised it to Vicky. 'Cheers! Happy birthday!'

The wine was ice-cold and delicious. It gave Jane an immediate alcohol rush and she started to feel more relaxed.

The noise level rose as more people crammed into the small space. A commotion by the door drew Jane's attention. A couple had just come in and were edging their way through the crush, trying to trying to find a free table. Jane stared in fascination at a tall, elegant young woman, taking in long slim legs in sprayed-on designer jeans, expensive leather jacket and impeccably styled blonde hair. Her eyes strayed to the man standing behind her. Her heart skipped a beat as she recognised the unmistakable figure of Liam Delahaye.

I don't believe it, she thought. *Why does he keep following me around?* As she watched, the girl draped herself around Liam and planted a kiss on his cheek. Jane noticed he looked embarrassed by the attention and hurriedly pulled his date over to sit down at the nearest table.

Jane turned back to Vicky's party. One of her guests had smuggled in a cake and now Alan, the landlord, was weaving his way through the crowd holding the pink and white confection aloft, all twenty-two candles blazing. A burst of applause and a raucous chorus of 'Happy Birthday To You' drew everyone's attention to their table. Jane caught Liam staring at her and determinedly turned away.

Minutes later Alan appeared at the table again, bearing a bottle of champagne and a tray of glasses. Vicky was flabbergasted. 'From the chap at the table by the door,' grinned Alan. 'To toast the birthday girl.'

Jane stared at Liam, who raised his glass to her, smiling sardonically.

'Wow! Who's that?' gasped Vicky. 'Friend of yours, Jane? Gorgeous, isn't he? He's hot!'

'That,' said Jane through gritted teeth, 'is the great Liam Delahaye. Lord Ashby's stud manager.'

'Bit of a stud himself, if you ask me,' giggled Vicky. Jason looked pained.

'Hey, Jane, what's up?' She gazed at her boss. 'Oh no!' She gave a mock groan. 'You like him, don't you? Don't you?'

Jane flushed. 'I do not! He's the most arrogant, cold, unfeeling man . . . '

'Yeah, yeah,' chortled Vicky. 'And I'm Paris Hilton's new best friend. You fancy the socks off him, even if you don't know it.'

'I'll go and get some more drinks.' Jane muttered, making her escape.

The pub dog was one of Jane's favourite patients. 'How's Rani?' she asked Alan as she leaned against the bar, aware of Liam's eyes on her, boring into her back.

'Oh, she's fine — a bit creaky with the arthritis, but that's to be expected, isn't it? Come through and say hello.' Alan lifted the counter top and Jane made her way into the back room.

An elderly Rottweiler lay snoozing in her basket by the fireside. She lifted her head and stared at Jane, then waggled her stumpy tail in recognition. Rani had the run of the bar after hours and was a very effective burglar deterrent. It would be a very brave — or desperate — thief who would risk coming face to face with a strange Rottie in a darkened building.

Jane crouched down and stroked the huge head. The dog grumbled softly in her throat, a greeting, not a threat.

'So,' said Alan. 'You've met Mr

43

Delahaye, I take it?'

Jane carried on petting the dog, her curtain of hair hiding her expression.

'Yes,' she admitted. 'He asked for my help with a horse.' She turned and looked up at Alan. 'Is he a regular here?' she asked casually. Alan could always be relied upon for gossip. 'Who's the blonde woman with him?'

'Ah, now — that's Lady Fenella Faraday!' Alan grinned at her, enjoying her feigned indifference.

'Lady Fenella?' Jane groaned. Not another of the unholy clan.

'Lord Ashby's granddaughter. That's why she's got a title. She's Edmund's cousin and he's got a huge chip on his shoulder about her having a title and not him. That's why he likes to throw his weight around, remind everyone he's the heir to the Estate.' He laughed. 'Got to feel a bit sorry for him, I suppose. Now Fenella, she's a bit of a wild one. Gossip is she's set her sights on Delahaye, even if he is just a member of staff. I can't imagine the old man would be too pleased about it, but she's used to getting her own way, that one.' He paused, not sure if he'd already said too much.

'Mind you,' he went on, 'if you listen to the old-timers who've been coming in here since the Flood, Miss Fenella was a regular tomboy when she was younger. Couldn't keep her away from her pony. Always the ringleader, getting her cousin Edmund into trouble. It's only since the pair of them left school that they've turned themselves into A-list celebs.'

'So what does the plain Mr Edmund do with himself all day? Does he have a job of any sort?'

Alan laughed. 'He was supposed to be going to college to learn how to run the Estate. But one gap year has turned into two, or three — rumour has it he hangs out at the fashionable clubs, trying to get in on the Royal Princes' circuit.' He looked thoughtful. 'Too much money, that's his problem. His mother seems to think that her responsibility for him ended when he turned eighteen and lets him do as he likes.'

Jane thought about her cosy relationship with her own mother, and couldn't help but feel sorry for young Edmund.

Alan went on, 'But Lady Fenella, now — Lord A is trying to get her interested in the horses again. Seems to think that working on the show horses with Liam might do the trick.'

Jane didn't want to hear any more. 'Excuse me,' she said, pushing her way to the door. 'Just popping off to powder my nose.'

Alan stared after her. 'Hey, Jane, you okay?' He shook his head. *Women!* he thought. He'd never understand them.

In the sanctuary of the Ladies, Jane splashed water on her flushed face and tried to control her thoughts. So that's how Liam knew so much about the family. He had a girlfriend. Fenella was Lord Ashby's granddaughter, and no doubt well-provided for in the old man's will. There was no competition.

Lady Fenella had it all: the looks, catwalk figure, and money.

Jane stared at herself in the mirror. The russet hair, which refused all her efforts with straighteners, cascaded to her shoulders in soft curls, caught back off her face with butterfly clips. Her low-cut sea-green top echoed the colour of her eyes, which she'd highlighted with creamy brown shadow and a touch of mascara. Her white trousers skimmed her hips, and gold sandals showed off the toenails she'd painted the same brownish pink as her lipstick. Not bad for an almost-thirty-year-old single mum. But up against a tall, willowy, aristocratic blonde — not a chance.

What does it matter anyway? she told herself fiercely. She had no interest in Liam Delahaye, and he certainly would not look at her in that way twice.

Jane made her way back to the table. She kissed Vicky and hugged her. 'Have a nice evening, Vicks,' she said. 'I have to get back. I'm on a promise to Callum not to be late.'

She escaped to the car park, trying not to draw attention to herself as she passed Liam's table. He was deep in conversation with the gorgeous Lady Fenella and appeared not to notice her.

As she rummaged in her bag for her keys, a voice behind her drawled: 'Running away, Miss Pardoe? Shame on you!'

Jane froze, then turned slowly, heart pounding. Liam was standing inches away, relaxed, confident, smiling down at her, thumbs in his belt loops. 'All dressed up tonight, Little Miss Vet. Who's the lucky fellow?' His eyes trailed lazily down her body and up again, coming to rest, deliberately, on her lips.

Jane stared at him, outraged. *The nerve of the man*, she thought.

'I don't live my entire life in jeans and sweatshirts, Mr Delahaye. And my private life is none of your business.'

He tut-tutted at her, waving a playful finger. 'Liam, please. I think we know each other well enough, don't you?'

What's going on here? thought Jane once more. *He's with that gorgeous woman, so what's he doing flirting with me?*

'It's Mrs Pardoe, if it's any of your business, and yes, I have a date this evening — with my son! And talking of dates, aren't you neglecting yours?'

His expression hardened. 'Very well, if that's the case, Mrs Pardoe, then I'll bid you goodnight.'

He stepped away from the car and watched as she drove away.

Liam stood for a moment, trying to get a grip on his emotions. He didn't want to admit how much Jane's revelation had affected him. She'd looked so adorable tonight, in that disturbing filmy top revealing a promise of a full, lush figure; and her angry, flashing sea-green eyes. He'd surreptitiously enjoyed the sight of her shapely hips in the clinging white trousers. He might even be persuaded to change his mind about that Titian hair. But what was she doing, going home alone to her

49

child? Where was the husband? Liam resolved to make it his business to find out more about Jane Pardoe.

He was not used to antagonism from his female acquaintances. He wanted to see this feisty young woman warm to him, to see those ocean-deep eyes look at him in quite a different way — and most of all, he wanted to caress those inviting curves.

'Foxy lady,' he breathed. 'Jane Pardoe, you're a foxy lady.' He took a deep breath, gazed up at the new moon rising above the trees, then turned on his heel and made his way back inside the pub to his date.

3

Sunday morning dawned. Jane had been hoping for a lie-in but Callum had other ideas. 'Come on Mummy,' he urged, bouncing on her bed. 'Get up.' Then he sat on her legs, pleating the duvet cover between his fingers. *How did he manage to have grubby hands so early in the morning?* Jane wondered. Small boys seemed to attract dirt like a magnet.

He gazed at her from under his long, blond lashes, wearing his most adorable expression. 'Come *on*,' he said again, impatiently. Jane laughed.

'Okay, you win. Off you go. I'll have a quick shower and you can make me some toast. I bet I'm down before it's ready!' Callum shot off the bed, laughing, aware that once again he'd come off best.

Jane stood under the shower, letting

the hot water cascade over her. She ran her soapy hands over her body, across her gently rounded stomach, letting her mind wander. She'd been toying with the idea of getting back together with Steve; now here she was in a turmoil, distracted by a cold, arrogant Irishman she'd met scarcely thirty-six hours earlier. She was behaving like a teenager with a pop star crush. She was a grown woman with her own business and a child to support.

The sensible thing would be to save her marriage, if she possibly could, and put stupid fantasies about Liam Delahaye firmly behind her. But how sensible was she? She closed her eyes, giving herself up to the caress of the warm water, dreaming of dark Irish eyes and the strong horseman's hands gentling the chestnut stallion . . .

'Mummy!' yelled Callum, banging on the shower cubicle. 'You've been ages! Your toast's popped up, I won, ha ha!'

The phone rang as Jane was up to her elbows in the washing-up. She waited for Cathy to pick up, then remembered her mother was out for the day. 'Callum,' she said, 'answer it for me, would you darling, and ask who it is?' She heard her little boy chatting on the phone while she hastily ran her hands under the tap and wiped them on her jeans.

'It's Mr Holiday, Mummy,' said Callum, handing her the phone. *Holiday?* thought Jane. *I don't know anyone called Mr Holiday.*

'Actually it's Delahaye,' said an amused, unmistakably Irish voice. 'Liam Delahaye.' Jane's stomach contracted. 'Good morning, Mrs Pardoe. Sorry to trouble you on a Sunday.'

Why on earth did I give him the idea I was still married? she thought miserably. 'What can I do for you, Mr Delahaye?' she said crisply. 'As you say, it is a Sunday and I am rather busy.'

'It's Sultan. Lord Ashby has asked if you could come and have another look? He's afraid the escapade yesterday with Mr Edmund may have done more damage than we thought.'

Jane thought for a moment, then made up her mind. If nothing else, she would be able to charge a hefty fee for a Sunday call-out.

'Okay, Mr. Delahaye.' She sighed. 'I'll be there as soon as I can.' She rang off, then realised she'd have to take Callum with her. *Too bad*, she thought. *He'll just have to accept I have other responsibilities in my life*. She gathered up her medical bag, checking the contents for essential supplies, then hesitated. She dashed upstairs, found her newest bootcut jeans and a pale grey hooded zip-up top, brushed her hair back under an alice band, slicked on a trace of lipstick, and finished off with a quick spritz of her favourite Ocean Breeze cologne. She looked at her reflection in the mirror. 'Ready as I'll ever be,' she muttered, and headed for the stairs.

'Callum!' she called. 'Get your trainers on. We're off to see Mr Holiday!'

As she opened the front door, Honey appeared, wagging her tail, anticipating a walk.'

'Can we take her, Mummy?' Callum adored walks with the dog.

Jane hastily weighed up the situation. It was a gorgeous morning and it didn't seem fair to leave the dog cooped up indoors. Maybe there'd be time for a quick visit to the common after she'd done what had to be done at the estate. Not that it would be anything other than another false alarm, she had no doubt of that.

'Come on, then. But she'll have to stay in the car until I say, all right?'

Callum hopped on to his booster cushion on the back seat. Jane checked his seat belt, then loaded Honey into the dog space at the rear.

As she drove through the country lanes, following the same route she'd taken just a couple of days before, Jane wondered at the strange course her life seemed to be taking. Last week she had simply been a professional woman, running her veterinary business, content with her life centred on her small son, living in peaceful harmony with her wonderfully supportive mum.

And now? A chance meeting with an attractive stranger had stirred up a morass of half-forgotten but not entirely unwelcome feelings, taking her out of her comfort zone and into uncharted territory. She couldn't deny that she was more than a little attracted to Liam. *Who wouldn't be?* she thought. On the one hand, here was a total stranger who only had to look at her with those dark, dangerous eyes and she was a quivering girl again, scared of her feelings yet wanting to get closer to him. On the other hand there was Steve, whom she'd known for most of her adult years, the father of her child and the only adult male Callum had known in his young life. The sensible, thing, she kept telling herself, was to work on her relationship with Steve, for Callum's sake. Given time, surely their love could be rekindled and she could put her dangerous fantasies firmly behind her.

The park looked quite different in daylight. Sheep grazed, their lambs skipping around them, jumping and bouncing in the spring sunshine. Callum was enchanted, laughing with delight at their antics, urging his mother to slow down so he could watch them. Jane was only too happy to oblige, wanting to put off as long as possible the moment when she'd come face to face with Liam again. At the back of her mind she'd been longing to see him, imagining what she'd say, how she would act towards him. And now here she was, dithering with nerves.

She scolded herself for being so silly. 'He's just a bloke,' she muttered under her breath. 'I've come to see the horse, not him.'

★ ★ ★

Liam was nowhere to be seen. Jane looked around, unsure what she should do. An elderly man in a well-worn tweed jacket and cord trousers shouted to her. 'Hey! Are you lost? This is private property, you know.'

Jane waited, sizing him up as he approached. The famous Lord Ashby. She recognized his voice.

'But I thought — ' She hesitated as Liam appeared from the hay barn. He looked a bit embarrassed, almost as though he had been caught out. She thought quickly. 'Lord Ashby? I'm Jane Pardoe, the vet who's been looking after Sultan. I was driving out this way and thought I would pop in to make sure the horse had suffered no ill-effects from his adventures yesterday.'

The old man looked her up and down, frowning behind his gold-rimmed spectacles, clearly not sure what to make of her. 'So you're the young woman I spoke to on the telephone? Delahaye tells me you've got your own practice. Fully qualified, he says, so I suppose you know what you're doing.'

Jane bit her tongue. Even in these days of supposed equality, she still came across this sort of chauvinistic attitude regularly, especially among men of his generation.

'I think you'll find Sultan's come to no harm under my care,' she said, smiling sweetly. 'I'd like to see him, if that's possible.'

Liam stepped forward, holding out his hand. 'Mrs Pardoe!' His voice was a bit too hearty, Jane thought. Yes, he'd been caught out. 'How good of you to call in, and on a Sunday, too. Do come with me — Sultan's out in the paddock keeping an eye on the mares.'

Jane took the proffered hand, registering the warm, dry palm and strong fingers tightening round hers. He drew her away from Lord Ashby, who looked on in mild surprise.

'What's this?' Jane hissed. 'You said his Lordship asked me to come!'

Liam smiled ruefully. 'Thanks for covering for me. I'll explain later. If you're staying, that is.'

Jane suddenly remembered Callum, sitting patiently in the car.

'It wasn't at all convenient having to come out this morning. I had to bring my boy with me. As I am here unofficially, I assume you don't mind if he comes with me? I'll vouch for his good behaviour.'

Before Liam could protest, Jane had freed Callum from the car, the dog tumbling out with him. 'Now just behave, please,' she warned him. 'Remember this isn't a play park. You can take Honey for a walk but she has to stay on the lead.' She turned to Liam. 'This is my son, Callum. Callum, this gentleman is Mr Delahaye.'

'Hello, Mr Holiday,' Callum chirped. He'd decided his version of this strange man's name was much more interesting.

Liam grinned and hunkered down beside the boy. 'Callum!' he said, ruffling the little boy's fair hair. 'Now isn't that a foine owld Oirish name, begorrah, to be sure!'

His broad music-hall Dublin accent made Jane laugh. 'I hadn't thought of it as being Irish, specially. We just liked the name. Simple as that.'

'We?' Liam raised an eyebrow.

'Me and Steve. Callum's dad. My husband.' She paused. 'To be strictly accurate, my ex-husband.'

Liam let out a long, slow breath. 'So, it's *Ms* Pardoe, then? Or just Jane?'

She looked up into his face. His peat-brown eyes crinkled in the sunlight, a slow pulse beat in his throat. His words hung between them. Somewhere nearby, a robin sang. It could have been an hour, an eternity, or just a few seconds. Time stood still in the pale spring sunshine.

Jane broke the silence. 'Liam — why did you pretend that Lord Ashby had asked to see me?'

He smiled then, a real, broad, pleased-to-be-with-you smile that turned Jane's legs to jelly. 'You want the truth? Quite honestly, Jane Pardoe, I just wanted to see you.' He paused, then went on, 'I think — in fact, I know — I made the wrong impression at the pub last night. I wanted to apologise. I don't want you to think badly of me.'

Jane held his gaze for a long moment, then, blushing, turned away. She wasn't quite ready for this new, gentle version of Liam Delahaye. She gathered her rapidly scattering wits together.

'I thought I'd come to see the horse,' she said briskly, trying to cover her confusion. 'Let's go.'

The path led them away from the busy yard through woodland, the trees misted with the palest lime green of the first leaves. Blackbirds and finches sang in the branches and dainty wild daffodils danced in the long grass beneath. In the distance, Jane glimpsed sunlight sparkling on water where the river took a wide, lazy bend in the final stages of its journey towards the estuary. Callum, holding Honey's lead, galloped ahead through the long grass, boy and dog enjoying their freedom after being cooped up in the car.

Jane walked in silence with Liam, their hands almost, but not quite, brushing. She was sure he must be able to hear the drum-beat of her heart. *What was he thinking?* she wondered. *Where was this leading?*

'Look!' he said suddenly. 'Sultan and his harem. Now isn't that a sight to gladden your heart?'

Sultan was grazing in a buttercup-gilded meadow, with just a post and rail fence between him and his three mares. Two young foals played in the sunshine, trying to get the hang of coping with their long, unruly legs. Jane caught her breath. The light glanced off the horses' shiny coats, Sultan's bright chestnut and two of the mares' different shades of bay and brown. The third one, heavily pregnant, was the prettiest little dapple grey Jane had ever seen. Grazing among them was a tiny black and white roly-poly Shetland pony, quite at home with the bigger animals.

'How gorgeous!' she breathed. 'They're beautiful, Liam.'

Her hand was resting on the top rail of the fence. He covered it with his own and squeezed, as if it was the most natural thing in the world. 'I've been around horses all my life,' he said. 'It's a dream come true to be looking after these fantastic animals.'

Jane smiled up at him. His Irishness shone through in his enthusiasm and showed her a different side of him. One, she was coming to realise more and more, she rather liked. But there was the other side, the over-confident, arrogant Liam. And she still didn't know where Fenella fitted in to the picture.

It was all too complicated! On the one hand there was the simple animal attraction she felt for him, woman to good-looking man. But she'd felt like this for Steve, hadn't she? She tried to convince herself again it would be best for Callum if she made an effort to get back with his dad.

Liam turned to look at her, searching her face with an intensity she'd not seen before, a question in his eyes. His step covered the short distance between them. He pulled her closer, his hand on her waist. The world spun on its axis, leaving her dizzy and breathless. Powerless to resist, she leaned in towards him, her whole being suffused with liquid fire as long-forgotten emotions revived. He ran a finger down her cheek, then turned her face up to his. Slowly, so slowly, he bent his head and gently brushed her lips with his. Sensing her acceptance he pressed more firmly, exploring her mouth with his own. For a few glorious moments Jane was in another world, where nothing existed but herself and her desire for this man.

With a supreme effort she pulled away. 'Oh!' she breathed, turning to avoid his gaze. 'Please, Liam, no.'

'What's wrong, Jane? I'm free, you tell me you're free. You know you wanted it, too. Tell me you didn't and I'll not bother you again.'

She gazed at him distrustfully. 'So what about your girlfriend, Lady

Fenella? Have you forgotten her? I'm not going to spoil a beautiful friendship, and besides, I — well, I hardly know you, Liam. And you don't know anything about me. And there's Callum . . . Callum!' Jane looked wildly about her. How could she have forgotten her son?

A shout and a dog's bark came from the woodland beyond the meadow. 'Callum!' she shouted. 'Where are you?'

A man appeared, herding Callum up the path in front of him, holding fast to Honey's lead. With a plummeting heart Jane recognised the tall, rangy figure of the young Edmund Faraday.

Callum ran to his mother. 'Mummy, Mummy, I wasn't being naughty, really I wasn't.'

Jane glared at Edmund. 'How dare you assault my son!' she spat at him, not caring if he was a lord, an earl or the heir to the throne. *A vixen defending her cub*, thought Liam admiringly. *Magnificent!*

Edmund, now sure of himself on his

own home patch, blustered, 'You, again! The woman with the dog that scared my horse. I might have known it. I found the boy wandering around in the woods. I don't know what he's been up to but we don't want strangers anywhere near the horses. Not with Sheba about to have her foal any day now.'

Honey pulled on her lead and whined, wanting this nasty man to release her. Liam intervened, retrieving the dog from Edmund's grip.

'Sir, it's probably my fault. Ms Pardoe called in to check on Sultan and with my permission, her son went off to explore the woods. I'm sure the dog has been on the lead the whole time, nowhere near the horses.' Liam went on, 'I absolutely agree that Sheba should be kept calm and it's more than my job's worth to allow any harm to come to her. I'm sorry if I have exceeded my authority.'

With Liam taking the blame, Edmund subsided like a leaking balloon, his anger dissipated. 'Oh, very well — no harm done this time, I suppose. But don't think I've forgotten about the incident on the common yesterday. Lucky for you I've decided to take it no further — for the moment.' He smiled unpleasantly at Jane. 'I could be persuaded to drop it altogether, you know. You only have to give the word.'

Jane stepped back, shocked at him repeating his proposition in public, and felt the heat of Liam's body close behind her.

'I'm sure you won't have any cause to complain again, sir,' he said, through gritted teeth. 'There'll be no need for any action on your part.' He held his clenched fists close to his sides, choosing his words carefully, clearly afraid of saying too much.

Callum, wide-eyed, pressed closer to his mother. He didn't understand what was going on, and didn't like it, but felt braver now he had Jane behind him. 'You're a nasty man!' he shouted to Edmund. 'Wait till I tell my dad!'

Jane exchanged a glance across the boy's head with Liam, then shook Callum by the shoulder. 'Come on, love,' she said as calmly as she could, her own anger still simmering just below the surface. 'No need for any of that. Let's get you home. I don't think we'll be needed here again.'

Jane held Liam's gaze for a long moment, then turned and walked with her boy and her dog back to the car.

The two men who stood watching them go had similar thoughts — but very different motives.

'She's not bad looking, for an older woman with a child,' Edmund mused. Liam hid his amusement at the youth's idea of an older woman. 'But I think I got off on the wrong foot with her. What do you reckon, Delahaye? Do you think if I played my cards right I'd be in with a chance?'

Liam bit his tongue. He realized Edmund Faraday had little or no experience with the opposite sex.

'I really couldn't say, sir. Don't you

think a girl nearer your age might be more your style? After all, as you say, Mrs Pardoe does have a small son as well as a demanding occupation. I think perhaps the — er — exciting social life you lead might be a bit too much for her.'

Edmund nodded gloomily. 'You're probably right. I'll see if Fenella can introduce me to one of her chums.' He straightened his back and shook himself out of his mood. 'And, talking of Fenella, I know my cousin. She's just playing with you, Delahaye. You're a step up from the stable boy she targeted last year, I grant you, but that's all you are — a bit of entertainment for a few weeks. You turned her head with that Irish brogue, and I suppose she finds you good-looking, but she'll tire of you soon enough — as soon as a rich, eligible marriage prospect appears on the scene.' Edmund smirked, knowing he had regained the upper hand.

Liam, too angry to trust himself to speak, turned on his heel and strode away through the woods. He knew from bitter experience that he needed to remove himself from the source of his anger. It was all too easy for him to let his temper boil over, with disastrous consequences. Now he was older and wiser, he had learned, with difficulty, to keep his mouth shut, walk away and let the fury pounding through his veins diffuse itself.

He headed for the river bank, where he would find solitude and a chance to let the impact of Edmund's weasel words flow away from him with the gentle ripple of the river. Sitting down on the sun-warmed turf, he looked around him at the timeless, peaceful scene. The dark green water was laced with starry white strands of early-flowering chickweed, and on the far bank the first clumps of bulrushes were thrusting their green spears upwards.

A pair of swans had built their nest on an island of reeds and he watched as the male bird fussed around the female, sitting patiently on her eggs. He dabbled in the water with his beak, finding tasty morsels.

Swans mate for life, he recalled. How long had these two nested here, successfully raising their cygnets, coming back to the same spot year after year? Not for the first time, he mused that the animal kingdom could teach humans a lot about family life, faithfulness and raising their young ones.

He wondered what had happened to end Jane's marriage. He assumed — hoped — she'd not been at fault. Yet he found it impossible to imagine any man abandoning such a beautiful, feisty woman and engaging young son.

Liam stared without seeing at the mesmeric, soothing motion of the water. His ready tongue had always been his worst fault, causing him problems at school — where he'd frequently been up before the Head and punished — and later in adult life. He'd been too close to losing it with Edmund, he knew; saying more than he should, landing himself in trouble.

In his heart of hearts, he knew he wasn't in love with Fenella. If he was honest with himself, he knew that Edmund was right; she was just amusing herself with him, as indeed he was with her, but they understood each other and he found her an entertaining companion.

He'd put to the back of his mind stories he'd heard bandied around the stable yard about her string of lovers, and he didn't care to know where or from whom she'd learned her beguiling tricks. He would go along with her games for as long as she wanted, yet when she tired of him, neither of them would be heartbroken.

He knew that Edmund was jealous of his success with women and although he was certain Jane had a healthy dislike for the young heir to the Ashby title, Liam was very afraid that he might do something foolish in an attempt to hurt her and restore his wounded pride.

Liam had been shaken by the

powerful feelings unleashed when he shared that brief kiss with Jane. He resolved to keep a very close eye on Edmund Faraday, and do everything in his power to keep Jane safe.

4

The telephone rang. Jane groaned. 'Why do people always call when we're eating? They must be psychic.'

'I'll get it!' Callum was off his chair in a flash. Jane and Cathy listened, smiling indulgently, as his little voice said clearly, 'This is Maybury PetCare. Can I help?' He was silent for a moment, then trotted back into the kitchen. 'It's for you, Mummy,' he said. 'It's Mr Holiday again.'

Jane dropped her fork with a clatter. 'Oh no!' she gasped. 'Now what does he want? Can't he leave me alone?'

Cathy looked puzzled. 'Who on earth is Mr Holiday?'

'It's not Mr Holiday, Mum, that's Callum's version of his name. It's Liam Delahaye from the Estate. I told you about him, remember?'

Jane took a deep breath and picked

up the phone. 'Liam. What can I do for you now? I hope nothing's wrong with any of the horses.'

She kept her voice as even and neutral as she knew how, although her heart was thudding. The deep Irish voice spread a warm blanket over her, friendly and beguiling.

'Hello, Jane — no, I don't have a sick animal for you this time. The fact is, I owe you an apology and I wondered if you'd let me buy you dinner? To say sorry for the unpleasant experience you had with Edmund Faraday.'

Jane was surprised into silence. This was heading into entirely new territory and she was not at all sure she wanted to go there.

'Jane? Are you there? Talk to me, please.'

'I — I don't know, Liam. I'm awfully busy right now, can I call you back?' Hurriedly Jane cut the call. Her hand was shaking.

Cathy looked at her in concern. 'What was all that about? I take it not a business call this time!'

'No, Mum, you're right. He wants to take me out to dinner, for goodness' sake. What do I do now?'

Cathy got up from the table and busied herself clearing the plates. Jane picked up a fork and traced the patterns on the tablecloth.

Callum sat on his chair, keeping very still and quiet. He knew they'd forgotten he was there and the conversation was about to get interesting.

'Look, lovey.' Cathy turned to face her daughter, a mixture of exasperation and sympathy on her face. 'Do you like this man?'

'Yes, but — it's complicated. I think he spells trouble.'

'Trouble? For you, you mean?'

'Well — okay, not exactly trouble, but he's getting in the way of my plans. I need to make an effort to see more of Steve, not go gallivanting off with a charming Irishman!'

Cathy laughed. 'Oh Jane, listen to yourself. How old are you — fifty?

You're an attractive young woman — you need to let yourself enjoy life a bit. If you want to have dinner with this Liam, then do it! It doesn't commit you to anything. He's not proposing marriage, is he?' Cathy paused for breath. 'Have some fun, Jane. If you don't want him, send him to me! From what you've told me about him, I wouldn't say no.'

Jane looked in mock horror at her mother. 'Oh, Mum! Honestly!'

'I hope you're not going to say 'at your age'!' Cathy teased. 'Maybe a handsome Irish toyboy is just what I need.'

Jane suddenly saw her mother through new eyes, and realised Cathy was an attractive woman still — with a few grey hairs and a bit on the plump side, but compared to other women of her age, quite capable of turning heads.

Callum risked putting in a word. 'I like Mr Holiday, Mummy. Can we go and see the horses again?'

Cathy grinned at Jane. 'There you

are. Out of the mouths of babes — the seal of approval, I would say. Ring him back, make a date.'

Jane held up her hands in mock surrender. 'Okay, okay, I get the message. But I'll leave it a bit. No point him thinking I'm too keen, is there?'

Jane dithered all evening, practising what she was going to say. But in the end it was surprisingly easy. Liam was friendly, charming and relaxed.

'You'll come? That's great, Jane. Tomorrow? Now what sort of food do you like? Italian? Chinese? You say — your choice.'

Jane thought quickly. She still wasn't sure she could trust Liam, and the thought of an intimate little restaurant with low lighting and hushed conversation was a bit intimidating.

'Actually, I'd like to go to the Ash,' she said, 'if that's all right with you. They do really good food there.'

Liam sounded surprised, maybe a little disappointed. 'If that's what you want, Jane, the Ash it is. I'll come and pick you up.' He put the phone down.

Too late she remembered the advertised folk music evening and hoped he wouldn't mind. *But he's Irish*, she reminded herself. *He's sure to like music, isn't he?*

★　★　★

Jane agonised for hours at work next day over what she was going to wear. Vicky got quite cross with her. 'It's a pub meal, Jane, not a banquet at the Ritz. You know you look good in most things. Just wear what you feel comfortable with. Now come on, you've got a waiting room full of sick animals. Concentrate!'

Jane sighed. 'You're absolutely right, of course, Vicks. Bring 'em on!'

Liam was early. Jane was upstairs in her bedroom, dithering over the contents of her wardrobe. 'Oh, no!' she muttered as she heard the bell ring. Opening her door a crack, she listened as her mother ushered Jane's date into the sitting room. She could imagine the conversation: Cathy bursting with curiosity, probably flirting a little, Liam, uncomfortable in the constraints of the small room, fielding her questions.

Jane swiftly zipped herself into the smartest pair of black trousers she possessed, added a cream-coloured cashmere sweater and at the last minute grabbed a rope of turquoise-coloured beads, which she knew brought out the colour of her eyes. *Don't try too hard*, she told herself. *You don't want him thinking he's important*. Make-up, she decided, should be kept to a minimum, her hair left curling loose on her shoulders.

Taking a deep breath Jane walked down the stairs as casually as her quaking knees would allow. She paused outside the sitting room, then opened the door. Liam was on the settee, with Honey's nose on his knee, chatting to Callum. He looked up at Jane and his face changed. She didn't realise she'd created exactly the sort of impression she was trying to avoid.

Liam saw a beautiful, natural young woman, fresh as a daisy and a million miles from the primped and pampered Fenella Faraday. He got to his feet and held out his hand. 'Well, hello!' he said softly. Jane felt herself blushing.

'You look nice, Mummy,' chirped Callum. 'Doesn't she, Mr Holiday?'

'She does indeed,' Liam replied. 'Gorgeous, I would say, Callum.'

Jane didn't dare look at Cathy. She felt every nerve tingling.

'Callum,' she said. 'It's time you had your supper. Come and give me a kiss — I'll come and tuck you in when I get back.'

She bent down and hugged the little boy, aware of Liam's eyes on her. Cathy led Callum away and Jane was alone with the Irishman.

'Let's go,' she said. 'We won't be able to park if we leave it too long.'

The Ashington Arms was even busier than usual, thanks to the added attraction of the folk band. The organisers were setting up the speakers on a small stage in the main public bar, and Jane was relieved to find that Alan had reserved a table for them in a quiet corner of the snug. Jane sat with her back to the wall, needing to feel the protection of the stonework behind her.

'Drink?' asked Liam. Jane chose her usual white wine. As Liam went to the bar, she caught Alan's eye and he gave her a surreptitious wink. Jane grinned at him, suddenly feeling better.

The Ash served good, wholesome pub food, nothing too fancy or unfamiliar to its loyal regulars. Jane knew the menu backwards but she pretended to study it, trying to collect her thoughts. She still couldn't quite believe she was here with Liam on what could only be described as a date.

Jane found she was enjoying herself. She gazed round at the familiar surroundings, taking in details she'd never really noticed before. The row of horse brasses, tacked to the oak beam above the bar, the row of stone cider jars, and a pile of books heaped on the windowsill, artfully arranged to look as if they'd been carelessly left there just a moment before. Jane knew she'd been right to choose to come here. The Ash was so well known to her, it was almost home-from-home and she felt safe and relaxed.

The wine helped her to unwind. The meal was delicious, and she tucked into her lasagna and salad with enjoyment. Liam observed her, amused, appreciating a young woman with a proper appetite. Jane, he thought, had a perfect figure. She wasn't always watching the calories, fretting about fitting into size zero clothes. Liam decided he preferred a woman to look like a normal healthy female, not a catwalk-thin supermodel.

'Mm, that was delicious.' Jane pushed her plate away. Liam smiled.

'More wine? Come on, Jane, you're not driving.' He topped up her drink. He'd had only one small glass. For a moment Jane wondered if he was trying to get her tipsy, but she rejected the thought as unworthy.

Alan came across to the table to clear their plates. 'Everything all right for you, Jane? Mr Delahaye?' he asked.

'Great, Alan!' Jane responded warmly. 'It always is.'

Liam leaned forward, arms on the table. 'Thank you for this, Jane. It's been a special evening for me.'

She gazed at him, not sure what exactly he meant. For a long moment their gaze held, dark eyes mirrored in jade green. Jane felt she was melting inside. Liam covered her hand with his own, his fingers interlacing with hers.

She pulled back, trying to control her feelings. 'Liam, I'm not sure where I stand with the Estate. I don't want to put myself or Callum in a situation where we might be made unwelcome by, um, any member of the family. And isn't Ashington on the Riverside vets' patch? The last thing I'd need, as a professional, would be for some other business to feel I was intruding on their ground.' She paused.

'And then there's Fenella. She's your girlfriend, isn't she? I've never been the sort to poach another woman's property. So where does all this leave me? You can see it's complicated. Three ways complicated.'

He stared at her, a small twitch at the side of his mouth. At that moment the band struck up, making conversation well-nigh impossible.

'Come on,' he shouted. 'Let's go. I need some air.'

He handed Jane into the car, then turned to face her, his features barely visible in the velvety darkness. He cupped her face in his hand, staring intently at her. 'Jane, oh sweet Jane, you say it's complicated for you. You've no idea what you're doing to me.' He sat up straight, facing her. 'Let's get some things straight. Riverside have no claim on the Estate. As far as I'm aware, Lord Ashby has never agreed that they should have sole rights. So on that score, there is no reason why you shouldn't come and look at the horses at any time.'

She started to speak.

'Yes, I know Edmund has taken a dislike to you, but I'm sure that is just his embarrassment at being caught out in a difficult situation. He's just a boy, immature for his age and not sure of where he stands at the moment.'

He fell silent briefly. 'But Fenella — well — okay, I've been tagging along with her for a little while. But trust me, Jane, there's never been anything between us. Nothing serious, any-way . . . '

Jane put a finger to his lips. 'Shush. It's okay, really.' She paused, then went on, 'But she does seem to think you're her property. So where does that leave me? I'm not going to be two-timed, Liam.'

'Fenella has the wrong idea, Jane. Believe me, she's the one making all the running. No, I'm not playing games with you. I can only hope Fenella gets the message — or moves on to somebody else!'

Jane sighed with satisfaction. She stretched out in the car, feeling warm and safe. 'Thank you for being so frank.'

She caught her breath as he reached for her hand and, very deliberately, kissed the tips of her fingers, one by one. His arm crept along the back of the seat, his hand playing with her hair, gently caressing her neck.

'Liam — ' she began, then her words were stifled as he drew her towards him and found her mouth in a kiss, softly at first, then with increasing intensity as she responded to him, yielding her lips to his, following his lead as her inhibitions were swept away. Somewhere in the back of her head a voice was telling her she had to be sensible, she ought to break away, but all her deepest instincts were urging her to go where this man was taking her, to recognise that he was the one she wanted.

Finally, with a great effort, she pulled away from him, her emotions in shreds.

'No, Liam, please,' she gasped. 'Just a friendly meal, you said. This isn't part of the deal.'

'Ah, sweetheart,' he murmured huskily, 'you're so beautiful. Look at you, all wrapped up in your sweater, like a young Colleen on her first date, trying to be good like she promised her daddy.' Passion enhanced his Irishness, wreaking havoc on Jane's senses. He sat back in his seat, and reached across for her hands. 'Come on, Jane, you know I'm mad for you. Can't we be more than just friends?'

Jane gazed into Liam's fathomless eyes, trying to collect her chaotic thoughts. She wanted him with every fibre of her being. But she still wasn't sure if she could trust him.

'No, Liam — I need to do what's best for my son. He needs his own father, someone who will be there for him, now and in five, ten years' time. I don't really know you, do I?'

She paused, searching for the right words. 'I'm very attracted to you, yes, I don't deny it. But . . . ' *Better the devil you know*, she added silently.

'Well, then — ' he urged.

'Liam, I know Steve. I was married to him for heaven's sake. I know he's the best thing for Callum. I admit we had our problems. He let me down badly, but he's changed a lot. And if I can work out some sort of relationship with him, then that's got to the best way. I'm sorry.'

Liam sighed. 'Well — if that's the way it's got to be, I suppose I'll have to accept it. But if it doesn't work out with your man, you'll know where I am.'

He paused, not quite ready to give up. 'There's no reason why we can't just be friends, is there? Real friends — no funny business, I swear. You'll still bring your boy up to the estate, won't you? I'll deal with Edmund, trust me. You won't have any bother with him.'

Jane's heart missed a beat. But she still didn't truly know where she stood on a professional level.

'Callum would love to see the

animals, that's for sure. I'd like us to be friends, Liam, truly I would. But you must promise to fix it with Lord Ashby. I don't want Riverside getting the wrong idea.'

He smiled at her, a friendly grin, uncomplicated and boyish. 'That's settled, then. From now on we're pals. Deal?' He stuck out his hand in a mocking gesture and she shook it, scarcely registering the gentle pressure on her fingers, or the second's extra delay before he released her.

5

The morning surgery was unusually quiet. 'I don't understand it, Jane,' Vicky commented. 'Monday morning is always so manic. Where is everybody?' She was perched on the high stool at the reception desk, shuffling bits of paper, doing some filing to keep herself occupied.

The early queue of clients with problems from the weekend had dwindled away. Jane ticked them off on her fingers. 'We had Sarah Brown's Westie with a bit of stick lodged in its throat, the tom cat from the farm with his ear torn again, Mr Davies with his granddaughter's rabbit and a couple of our weight-watchers in for a check-up. That's about it. Odd, isn't it? Maybe all our animals have suddenly become fit and healthy!'

She laughed, but Vicky could tell she was puzzled. 'Oh well, let's try and enjoy the peace and quiet. It's bound to pick up soon, and then we'll be rushed off our feet again.'

★ ★ ★

'You look all in, lovey,' commented Cathy that evening. She knew Jane was worried about the downturn in business, and had been sleeping badly. Worryingly, she'd heard that Riverside were offering special deals to new clients and several of Jane's best customers had defected to the new practice with its modern facilities and bright young vets.

'You're right, Mum. I'm exhausted. I fancy a nice long bath and an early night. But I've got to have a go at the accounts tonight.'

'Mummy,' ventured Callum. 'Can you help me with my Lego? It's gone all funny.' He was sitting on the floor with a heap of small coloured bricks, frowning at the printed instructions on the box.

Jane looked up from the kitchen table, where she was surrounded by a paper mountain of invoices, bills and the occasional receipt. She punched some numbers into her calculator and scribbled the figures down. 'Sorry, darling, I've got to do these sums, then I'll have a look. Can Grandma help?'

'She's hopeless. I need you. Or Dad,' he muttered.

Jane felt guilty. She knew she'd been neglecting her son, but her problems with the business had overruled everything else.

Cathy regarded her stressed-out daughter. 'You know the answer, don't you? Ask Steve. He's an accountant. He should be able to find a way out.'

Jane knew she was right. But Steve had been so sure she wouldn't be able to succeed in running her own business, she didn't want to have to admit she was in trouble.

'I'll think about it. Promise.' She pushed the muddle of papers into an untidy heap and, yawning widely, stretched her arms above her head. 'Come on, Callum, let's have a look at this building of yours.'

★ ★ ★

Next morning she phoned Steve's office. 'Can I speak to Mr Pardoe, please? It's his — er — it's Jane Pardoe here.'

The receptionist was her usual snooty self. 'I'll see if he's free, Mrs Pardoe. I'll just put you on hold.'

Jane was fidgeting, trying to decide what she was going to say to Steve, and in no mood to listen to Hits from the Musicals. Especially not a track of *If I Were a Rich Man*. She drummed her fingers.

'Jane! This is a surprise — what can I do for you?' Jane jumped as Steve's voice cut into the music. 'Nothing wrong with my boy, I hope?'

Keep calm, she told herself. *Don't rise to the bait.*

'No — Callum's fine. I was hoping

you could give me some advice if you could spare the time. You could come to the house one evening, maybe?'

'Well, I am very busy just at the moment, but I think I could find you a window on — hmmm, let's say, Thursday? Around seven-thirty?'

Jane stifled a giggle at his choice of words. Steve never used to be so pompous. 'That would be just fine,' she answered. 'Come to supper. Callum will be pleased to see you.'

* * *

She couldn't put it off any longer. The supper things had been cleared away; Callum was tucked up in bed, having enjoyed the rare treat of a bedtime story read by his dad; Cathy had retreated to the sitting room to watch TV and Jane now sat at the kitchen table, confronting Steve.

'It's the business,' she started, then paused, seeing the beginnings of a smirk appear on his handsome face.

'Please, Steve, I don't want any I-told-you-so comments. This really is not my fault. At least, I don't think it is.'

Steve pulled out his calculator and a notebook and leafed his way through the pile of bills and receipts. Jane watched him in silence, hoping against hope that he'd find some loophole she'd not noticed.

After a while he looked up. He leaned back in his chair, cleared his throat and puffed out his cheeks. 'Hmmm. I'm sorry, old girl, you do seem to be in a bit of a fix.' Jane's heart sank. 'Tell you what, why don't I take some of this stuff away with me and have a proper look at it when I've got more time? Have a word with a couple of people, see if I can come up with something that might bail you out? That's the best I can do at the moment.'

He smiled at Jane. 'There's always a way out, even if it's not what you expect.' He looked at his watch. 'Ah well, it's getting late. I need my beauty sleep, even if you don't!'

He gathered the papers into a large envelope and strode towards the door calling a cheery 'Goodnight' to Cathy.

Jane walked with him to his car.

'I'll ring you,' he said as he slid into the lush leather interior. He turned the ignition and the powerful car purred into life. 'Don't worry, Janey, something will turn up.'

Jane watched him go, emotions playing havoc with her rational mind. He was so right for Callum, and in spite of his money, his lifestyle and his blond good looks, she realised, so very wrong for her! *Damn you, Liam Delahaye*, she thought, *messing up my plans*. She'd have to try to forget him if Steve was going to figure in her life again.

Steve phoned a few days later. 'I think we should meet up,' he said, 'away from the house. What do you say?'

'It's your day with Callum on Sunday,' she ventured. 'Perhaps we could take him to a beach somewhere, let him play while we talk.' *Fingers crossed*, she said to herself. Surely he'd agree this time.

★ ★ ★

It was a glorious day. Steve picked them up, smiling indulgently as Callum piled his football and bucket and spade into the boot of the immaculate car, along with a bundle of towels and swimming costumes, and the picnic Jane had been up since dawn preparing.

'Not the dog,' he insisted. 'I take clients out in this car, Janey. I can't have dog hairs all over the seats.'

Honey watched mournfully as they drove away.

The trip across the harbour on the car ferry was a special treat for Callum. He loved the clanking of the chains as the little vessel hauled its cargo of holidaymakers and local business traffic across to the windswept heathland of the Isle of Purbeck. He got out of the car with Steve, standing on the passenger deck as the slipway receded behind them. Jane watched, amused, as Steve eyed up the millionaires' mansions fronting the water, each with its own deepwater mooring for yachts and jet skis. *Rich boys' toys*, she thought. She knew how Steve yearned for a part of that lifestyle. A flotilla of small sailing boats played dodge with the bulky, slab-sided ferry, trying to get into the harbour on the incoming tide, and a couple of big, expensive-looking power boats muscled past, unwilling to wait their turn.

Steve found a deserted beach, a world away from the cosmopolitan bustle of Bournemouth, ignored by ice-cream sellers and sunbed providers. The tide was on the turn, retreating from the high water mark leaving behind a ribbon of jade green seaweed and a tumble of dainty pastel-coloured shells, some as tiny and translucent as babies' finger nails. There was no wind. The water rippled lazily on to the sand and receded, leaving the beach pristine, ridged and firm, perfect for walking barefoot.

Callum whooped with delight and raced off ahead, chasing his ball and splashing in the shallows. Jane kicked off her flipflops and curled her toes into the water, loving the sudden rush of cold.

'Dad, play football with me!' Callum was insistent. With the game underway, Jane found a sheltered spot by the sand dunes and spread a towel on the sand. She watched father and son for a while, then let her eyes roam out to sea, and back to the far end of the bay.

A moving figure caught her attention, shimmering in the bright sunlight. As she watched, trying to puzzle out what it could be, she realised it was a horse, ridden bareback. Sparkling silver shards of light glanced off the water as the horse cantered through the shallows. With a catch of her breath, Jane recognised the big chestnut stallion. And the rider, sitting easily on its back, relaxed, right hand loosely holding the reins, the other resting on his thigh.

Sultan — and Liam! What on earth was he doing, way out here? With any luck he wouldn't notice her.

Liam, seeing there were people on the beach ahead of him, slowed the horse to a walk as the football came bouncing towards them. The horse shied away and splashed into deeper water, soaking its rider. Jane watched, trying not to laugh.

Callum, retrieving the ball, shouted, 'It's Mr Holiday, Mummy!'

Liam looked around him and spotted Jane, up by the sand dunes. Reluctantly she got to her feet and walked slowly down the beach, uncomfortably aware of her skimpy vest top and shorts. Liam slipped from Sultan's back and waited, not moving, dark eyes roaming over her half-clad body as she approached him. His soaking wet jeans clung to his thighs, playing havoc with her emotions.

'Who is this?' Steve's voice, edged with irritation, broke into the silence. 'Who is this man, Jane? How come

Callum knows him?' He stared at the newcomer, taking in the man's tanned, muscular physique and dark good looks.

Jane stammered, 'Steve, this is Liam Delahaye, from the Ashington Estate. I've been treating this horse for him. Callum came with me — nothing to tell, really. Liam, this is Steve Pardoe. My — er — Callum's father.'

The two men looked at each other with mutual dislike.

'Steve's been looking at my business accounts,' Jane explained. 'He's going to advise me on what to do.'

Liam stared at her. 'Well, that's grand then, Mrs Pardoe. He's the right man to sort you out, I don't doubt.' With one fluid movement he vaulted back on to the horse and gathered up the reins. 'I'm sorry to have interrupted your family day out.' He patted the horse's neck. 'Lord Ashby thought a drop of seawater would be good for Sultan's legs, so we came down here for a paddle.'

Suddenly Jane found she couldn't bear to let him go. 'Liam — I've been wondering — how's Sheba?'

'Ah, sure, Sheba's just grand. You'll be coming up to see her yourself soon?' His stare was direct, challenging.

Jane blushed, feeling wrong-footed again.

'Maybe — I don't know, Liam. We'll see.'

'Don't let us keep you.' Steve's voice cut in. Jane had almost forgotten he was there. 'Come along, Callum. Let's finish our game.'

* * *

The picnic was demolished and packed away. Callum was busy constructing a huge sandcastle, and now Jane couldn't put it off any longer. She hated having to ask for Steve's advice, to admit her business was in trouble, but she realised there was no alternative.

'So, what do you think about my books, Steve?' she asked. 'Is there anything I can do to improve things?'

Steve was silent, not looking at her, turning over the warm, dry sand with his hands, allowing it to trickle through his fingers. *Just like my business is trickling away*, thought Jane with a lump in her throat.

Presently he dusted off his hands and reached into his back pocket. 'You'd better read this,' he said. 'You won't like it, but as far as I can see it's your best option, with things as they stand.' He dropped the envelope in her lap, then stood up and went to help Callum with his castle.

It was a white business envelope bearing, Jane noticed with unease, the Riverside Practice logo. It was addressed to her. She held it in her hands for a long moment, then slit it open.

The letter was expertly typed, businesslike, signed with a flourish in black ink. Jane read it through, disbelieving, then again, with a growing sense of desperation. Her head was spinning;

she couldn't think clearly. Surely this wasn't the only way out?

Steve came back to her and dropped down by her side. 'So what do you think? As your financial adviser I would recommend you to think carefully about the offer.'

'But, Steve, this is terrible! Is there really no other way out for me?'

'Well, Janey, you don't *have* to accept their offer. But in my opinion you'd only be prolonging the agony if you didn't.'

'But to sell out to *them*, Steve — you're suggesting I give it all up, abandon my dream without a fight! How can I do that? My own business — it's what I've always wanted. You know that.'

Steve took her hand. She stiffened, his touch not welcome.

'Janey, Janey — '

'Don't call me that! You know I hate it.'

'Jane, what Riverside are offering is to buy you out and for you to become part of their organisation. You'd have to give up your independence, that's part of the deal, but you'd have their backing and you could stay in your premises, and maybe keep Vicky on.' He paused. 'But they might want to replace her with one of their own people.'

Jane was close to tears. On the face of it, Riverside's offer did make a lot of financial sense. But to expect her to sell out to them, was too much to ask. And how could she possibly tell Vicky she'd have to go?

'I can't make this sort of decision right now, Steve,' she muttered, almost too choked up to speak. 'I'll have to think about it carefully. There's an awful lot for me to take in.'

'Just don't leave it too long, Janey — Jane,' he corrected himself. 'They won't wait for ever.'

6

Jane's head was in turmoil. She'd been unable to sleep since Steve had dropped Riverside's bombshell letter into her lap. She lay awake at night turning over in her mind the pros and cons of their offer.

On the face of it, it would make perfect sense for Maybury PetCare to become part of the Riverside Practice. She would be joining a team of experts with all the back-up she needed. The surgery would have a total makeover, the equipment replaced with the best that money could buy.

On the other hand, she'd lose her independence. She would have no say over the day-to-day running of the surgery. And there was Vicky. As a trained veterinary nurse, Vicky was a great asset. But Steve had hinted the Riverside bosses might want to replace her with one of their own, more highly-qualified people. Vicky was a friend first, and valued employee second. How could Jane do without her? Meanwhile, the bills had to be paid. She had to make a living for her family.

Cathy had urged her not to be too hasty, not allow herself to be panicked into a decision she'd regret for the rest of her life.

Vicky was just as positive. 'We're all in this together, Jane,' she said. 'If it would help, I'd be happy to work on Saturdays. I don't suppose Riverside have a Saturday surgery, do they?'

Jane hugged her. 'Vicky, you're the best friend a girl could wish for.'

Cathy came up with her own plan. 'I'll organise a little shop,' she declared. 'We could use that back store room — clear it out and sell some of those big bags of dried dog food, and cat litter — things people find difficult to haul back from the supermarket. And fancy collars and leads, hamster wheels and things. Leave it to me, Jane. I'll be glad to have a project.'

Jane, concentrating on saving her business, hadn't seen or heard from Liam since the day they had met on the beach. Even though she knew she was doing the right thing by keeping clear of him and the Estate, there was a great, gaping hole in her heart that Steve couldn't come close to filling, even though she was trying her best to warm to him once more.

It would be so much easier, she mused sadly, if she'd never met the Irishman. Steve had been all that she thought she ever wanted, once; surely he could be so again?

* * *

The surgery was buzzing. Jane and Vicky were happy to see Maybury PetCare busy. The Saturday clinic was proving popular, and Cathy's shop was going from strength to strength.

Even so, Steve had stepped up his

campaign for Jane to sell out to Riverside. 'You may be doing okay for now,' he warned, 'but it can't last, you know. There's no way you can survive on your own. Small businesses like yours fail every week. The longer you put it off, the worse it will be.'

Cathy was concerned, too. 'You're working much too hard, my love. The hours are too much for one woman on her own — yes, I know you've got Vicky, but you're the only qualified vet.'

Jane knew she had a point. She felt guilty about asking Vicky to give up her Saturdays, but her loyal friend brushed off Jane's misgivings.

'I'm happy to be here, honestly, Jane. Let's hope we've turned the tide and things will get easier.'

Not without taking on another fully-trained vet, Jane thought, and there was no way the business could afford such a luxury.

* * *

The insistent ringing of the telephone dragged Jane from exhausted sleep. She was tempted to ignore it, but, knowing it was probably some animal in trouble, she groped for the handset.

'Jane.' Liam's voice snapped her into alertness. 'It's Sheba. You must come, quickly!'

The yard was in darkness, just as it had been on Jane's first visit to Ashington. Liam was in the loose box with the mare, which was about to give birth. Liam gave her a swift glance and a brief nod. 'Thank goodness! Lord Ashby's away, and I didn't want to cope on my own.'

The filly foal's birth appeared to be quick and easy, and Jane smiled with pleasure at the new little life. Then, in a heart-stopping moment, she realised the foal wasn't breathing. Swiftly she cleaned its nose and mouth, opened the tiny jaws and delivered mouth-to-mouth resuscitation, whilst Liam massaged the little limp body with a wisp of straw to stimulate circulation.

After a tense few moments, the foal coughed and sneezed and opened its eyes. Sheba bent her head and whickered softly to her new daughter, nudging her gently with her nose. Jane breathed a heartfelt prayer of thanks.

'There you go, Liam,' she said wearily. 'She'll be fine now. Let me know if you need me again.'

He looked at her, properly, for the first time that night, deep into her eyes.

'Oh, Jane!' he said softly. 'Thank God you were here. You've no idea how much this little mare and her foal mean to his Lordship. And you've no idea how very much you've come to mean to me.' He drew her to him and kissed her gently — like a friend, not a lover.

With tears in her eyes, Jane drove away.

7

Callum was standing on the paddock rail, eagerly inspecting the new foal. 'What's her name, Mummy?' he asked.

The unmistakable Irish voice behind them made Jane jump. 'It's Kismet.'

Her heart did a double flip and she turned slowly. Liam was standing a little way off, watching her. Jane went weak at the knees at the sight of him, tall and tanned, dark hair falling over his forehead. And he was smiling his special smile for her.

Liam moved to lean on the fence beside Callum, dropping a gentle hand on the boy's shoulder. 'So young man, what do you think of our new baby?'

Callum tore his gaze away from the foal and glanced up at the tall man by his side. 'I think she's great, Mr Holiday. Do you know my mummy helped her to be born?'

'I do indeed. Your mummy was a lot of help. She's a very good vet.'

Jane blushed scarlet. 'Liam,' she said, 'why did you call me out, not one of the Riverside people? You must know they would have more experience than me.'

'Ah, but you have a real instinct for horses, and that's something all the qualifications in the world can't teach you. And Lord Ashby knows it, too.' He smiled at her, his dark eyes speaking volumes.

Jane returned his gaze, unable to conceal her own message.

'Mr Holiday,' said Callum, feeling left out of the conversation. 'What's the name of the other little horse?' He pointed to Kismet's playmate, the tubby piebald Shetland pony, determinedly munching his way through a clump of buttercups as if he didn't know where his next meal was coming from.

'That's Jigsaw. Lord Ashby's grand-children used to ride him when they were around your age, Callum. Lady

Fenella and her sister used to spend their summer holidays here, as well as their cousin, Edmund Faraday. Jigsaw was their playmate.'

'What does he do now?'

'Now? Well, most of the time he just stays here in the paddock, playing with the foals and eating too much!'

'Doesn't he get bored?'

Liam laughed. 'Well, he doesn't say much. But yes, I suppose he does get a bit bored. He needs some exercise. There's nobody to ride him now, so I take him for walks when I can find the time. Like you take Honey for walks.' Jane heard his voice change and he glanced at her over Callum's head, the germ of an idea sparking between them. Their eyes met, held, and from the cinders Jane thought had been extinguished, the flame caught fire again. In spite of herself she moved closer to him, wanting, longing for contact — any contact — with him. Neither of them spoke. They both recognised what had happened. No

116

words were necessary.

Lord Ashby provided a welcome interruption. He sauntered down the path towards them, every inch the aristocratic lord of the manor. 'Good morning, Mrs Pardoe! Come to see how your filly's doing, I presume?'

Jane shook his outstretched hand. 'It's good to see you, Lord Ashby. And good to see the pair of them looking so well.'

Lord Ashby smiled at her. 'I can't thank you enough for what you did. Actually, you've saved me a phone call. I have some news that might interest you and I was going to ask you to come up to the Hall for a chat.' He glanced at Callum, happily chattering away to Liam. 'But what are we going to do with your boy? He'd be very bored, hanging about up at the house.'

Jane had an idea.

'Callum,' she said, 'I need to go and have a talk with Lord Ashby. Will you be a good boy and stay with Mr Holiday for a little while? I think he might have a job for you.'

Liam looked down at the boy. 'How about you and me taking Jigsaw for that walk we were talking about?'

Jane laughed at her son's eager expression. 'I think that's a 'yes' then, Liam. Off you go, Callum, you'll need to get Jigsaw ready.'

The small blond boy and tall dark man walked off towards the yard, deep in conversation. Lord Ashby watched them, with the suspicion of a frown creasing his brow.

Jane felt a shiver of excitement as she followed Lord Ashby up the imposing stone steps of the Hall, and into the impressive entrance hall. Not wanting to look like a gawping tourist, she allowed herself a brief glance around, taking in the wide black and white marble tiled floor, the graceful stone columns holding up the soaring painted ceiling, the classic glass dome in the roof, which flooded the space with light.

She followed Lord Ashby through to

the back of the hall, into a cosy study, furnished with a large antique desk and deep, inviting chairs upholstered in dark green leather.

She sneaked a quick look around the small cluttered room. Bookshelves crammed with volumes reflecting Lord Ashby's interest in everything to do with the countryside, family photographs on every surface. Regimental memorabilia from his time in the Army. A lingering scent of woodsmoke hung in the air, although at this time of year there was no fire burning in the grate. Jane could imagine that in winter this would be a snug little cave, a sanctuary away from the chilly, formal rooms in the rest of the house.

He sat down at his desk and rearranged some papers, adjusted his glasses and cleared his throat. 'Coffee?' he asked, and without waiting for a reply, tugged at an old-fashioned bell-pull at the side of the fireplace. After a few moments the door opened to reveal a small, neat woman clad in an overall, wiping her hands on a tea towel. Jane willed her to say 'You rang, m'lord?' and hid her amusement behind her hand.

But she was disappointed. 'Yes?' the woman snapped. 'What is it?'

To Jane's amazement Lord Ashby seemed almost afraid of his housekeeper. 'Ah, Delia, I'm sorry to drag you from your kitchen, but could we possibly have coffee? And some of your delicious flapjack, if it wouldn't be too much trouble?'

Delia pursed her lips and heaved a put-upon sigh. 'Well,' she said. 'Don't blame me if the cheese souffle's ruined.' She let the door bang behind her as she bustled out.

Lord Ashby turned to Jane with a rueful smile. 'I'm afraid Delia rules the domestic arrangements of the house these days. She tries to rule me, too, but I don't know what I'd do if she left. Now, when my wife was alive . . . ' He shuffled the papers on his desk, collecting his thoughts.

'Now, Jane — may I call you Jane? —

down to business.' He selected a dauntingly legal-looking document from the heap on his desk. 'I've been reviewing my plans for the Estate. I'm being pressurised by another firm of veterinary surgeons and, as a result, I've asked my solicitor to draw up a formal contract —'

Jane's heart sank.

' — to give you sole rights to treat all the horses on the Ashington Estate.' He paused. 'And we will, of course, pay you a monthly fee so that we can call you out at a moment's notice.'

The sum he mentioned made Jane's head spin.

She stared at him, not quite able to believe what she was hearing. 'Delahaye told me all that you did to save Sheba's foal. There's no one I would rather trust with my horses. So if you agree to the terms, Jane, just sign here.' He pointed with his pen.

In a daze, she signed her name on the paper and, stammering her thanks, Jane pushed back her chair. Lord Ashby stopped her.

'I just wanted to say one more thing, my dear.' The expression on his face troubled her. 'I have the impression you're getting close to Delahaye.'

She nodded, unable to deny it.

'Be careful, Jane. I wouldn't want either you or your boy to get hurt. Liam has — unresolved issues, shall we say. Just watch your step.'

Jane headed across the hallway, the signed contract clutched in her hand. She still couldn't quite take in what had happened. Had Lord Ashby really just sorted all her business problems for her? Yesterday she'd been on the verge of phoning Steve to tell him that she'd accept Riverside's offer to buy her out. Now, she was free to run her practice the way she wanted, and employ an assistant to take some of the workload. But there was the strange warning he'd given her about Liam. She couldn't imagine what he meant.

As she reached the doorway, she had the unmistakable feeling of being watched. Slowly she turned and stared back into the hallway. A cloud passed across the sun, cutting the light coming down from the dome. A slight movement caught her eye. She froze, rooted to the spot. At the top of the stairs Edmund Faraday was watching her, motionless as one of the statues in the hall. As she stared at him, he started down the stairs towards her. Whirling round, she made her escape into the sunlit garden.

*　*　*

She found Callum in the stable yard with Liam. The Shetland, Jigsaw, was tied up to a ring set in the wall and Callum was having a lesson in how to groom a small, hairy pony. Black and white hairs went flying in all directions as Callum energetically applied the brush to the pony's flanks.

'Hi, Mummy!' he called. 'I'm helping Mr Holiday get all of Jigsaw's winter coat off. We're making him all nice and shiny, like the big horses.'

123

'He's doing a grand job here, Jane.' Liam was standing back, supervising but not interfering, letting Callum do the work. The little animal stood patiently, dozing in the sunshine, apparently enjoying the boy's efforts.

Jane leaned against the stable door, watching her son so happily occupied, engrossed in his task. Her nerves were still jangling from her latest encounter with Edmund Faraday. The way he'd been watching her from the top of the staircase, silent, unmoving, had bothered her more than she cared to admit. She had thought all her problems were over, now that Lord Ashby had given her a contract to work on the Estate, but Jane realised she might still have problems with the younger members of the family.

'What's the boy doing with that animal?'

Jane jumped. Speak of the devil!

Edmund sauntered into the stable yard, ignoring Jane. 'Delahaye, you've no business allowing just anybody near our horses.'

Jane forgot her nerves and squared up to the bully. 'Mr Faraday, I don't know what it is about me and my family that makes you hate us so much. Liam Delahaye was merely amusing my son whilst I had a conversation with Lord Ashby. And the pony needed grooming, surely you can see that? I don't suppose you were about to do it yourself.'

Faraday gaped at her, lost for words, unused to being spoken to in that way. He moved a step closer. 'Mrs Pardoe, we don't need you here. I'll see you banned from this estate, if it's the last thing I do!'

Lord Ashby arrived on the scene in time to hear this last threat.

'I don't think so, Edmund. Calm yourself. It's unseemly for a man in your position to make such an unedifying spectacle of himself.'

Faraday glowered at his uncle. 'I'm only trying to protect your interests. We can't have just anybody coming in and messing about with the horses.'

'Very commendable, Edmund, and normally I would agree with you. However, quite unnecessary in this instance. Mrs Pardoe has just signed a contract which makes her the official veterinary surgeon for my horses.'

'But . . . but . . . but . . . ' Edmund was lost for words. He gaped at Lord Ashby, mouth opening and closing like a fish, completely floored by his uncle's announcement. 'This woman?' he gasped. 'In charge of Sultan and the others? Why wasn't I consulted? Or Fenella? Have you totally lost the plot, Uncle George?'

Lord Ashby regarded his heir coolly. 'It was my decision, mine alone. I happen to have a high regard for Mrs Pardoe's skill with horses, and so should you, Edmund.'

Jane had a sudden, unexpected pang of sympathy for the young man. He was Lord Ashby's heir, but apparently he hadn't a clue about the job he was to take on, and unable to match up to his uncle who had served with distinction in the Army and ran the estate so efficiently. Any authority Edmund tried to wield was countermanded by the old man, who was clearly not intending to hand over the reins any time soon.

Jane stole a glance at Liam. He was standing back, away from the argument, an unreadable expression on his face. She wondered if he'd had any influence in Lord Ashby's decision.

Edmund tried to regain the upper hand. 'We'll see what my cousin has to say about this.' He glared at his uncle, turned on his heel and strode away. Slowly the highly-charged atmosphere in the stable yard began to dissipate.

Lord Ashby turned to Callum, standing behind his mother, hiding from the nasty man. 'Now then, young feller, what about this pony? You can't leave the job half done, you know.' He picked up the brush and handed it back to Callum. 'Off you go.'

He nodded to Jane, and marched briskly back to the house.

In a dream Jane went to Liam and found herself folded in his arms. He dropped a kiss on the top of her head. 'So who's flavour of the month, then?' he teased. 'Lord Ashby's official vet, no less.'

He looked down at her, suddenly serious. 'Be careful, Jane,' he warned. 'Mr Edmund's furious, and Lady Fenella won't be pleased either. They can still cause mischief, those two. Just watch your step.'

* * *

Jane phoned Steve after supper, happily anticipating his pleasure at her unexpected good news. Cathy had been thrilled and excited, seeing all kinds of possibilities opening up for Jane now that she had Lord Ashby's support.

Vicky's reaction, too, had been predictable. 'That's absolutely brilliant, Jane. But I won't ask what you had to do to get his Lordship on your side! And none of it has anything to do with the hot Irishman, I suppose?'

'That's outrageous, Vicky! No, Liam had nothing to do with it. He was as surprised as anyone. But I'm going to make the most of this chance. Just you watch me!' Still on Cloud Nine, Jane waited for Steve to pick up.

'Steve! I've got some incredible news.' She poured out the whole story. 'So you see, I can tear up Riverside's letter. Now I can make it on my own. Even pay for a qualified assistant. Isn't it wonderful?'

His response was completely unexpected.

'You stupid woman!' he yelled. 'You've ruined everything. I promised them you'd . . . ' His voice tailed off.

Jane went cold. 'You promised who, Steve? Promised what? What are you talking about?'

He was too furious to care what he was saying. 'Oh, I don't suppose any of it matters now. You might as well know the truth. Riverside had promised me a big bonus if I delivered you and your tatty little business to them. You were more of a threat to them than you realised. Now you tell me you're the Ashington vet. Well, that's just dandy for you, Janey, just dandy. Thank you very much.' He thumped the phone down.

Her hopes for a future with Steve in ruins, Jane, in shock, burst into tears.

'Don't call me Janey,' she whispered.

8

Jane threw herself into her work. The bombshell of Steve's betrayal had hurt her more than she cared to acknowledge. All she could hope for now was that she'd be able to maintain some sort of contact with him, for Callum's sake. Any thoughts of a future as a family were dead and buried.

Edmund and Fenella Faraday watched with increasing disquiet as Jane and her son became part of Liam's life. Edmund hadn't forgotten his first encounter with Jane when she'd turned down his advances.

'Snooty little cow,' he growled. 'Who does she think she is? I promised I'd get back at her, and I will one of these days.'

Fenella regarded him coolly. 'Is she really worth the effort, cousin? As you say, she's nothing special. In your position, with your money and title, you could have anyone you wanted. So why beat yourself up over that very ordinary young woman?'

'You can talk. You want her out of the picture so Delahaye will come running back to you. Face it, Fenella, you don't really want him, do you? Your pride's hurt. You just like a bit of rough from time to time.'

She grimaced. 'Honestly, Ed, for a man who had such an expensive education, you really are awfully coarse sometimes. My 'bit of rough', as you so charmingly put it, does have certain — attributes — that I've found sadly lacking in other more elevated social circles.'

'Hmmm. Well, if you don't want those attributes enjoyed elsewhere, we'd better do something about it. Leave it to me.'

* * *

The first rays of the sun were gilding the tops of the trees as Jane slipped quietly out of the house and drove along the deserted lanes towards the Estate. The butterflies in her tummy were getting hard to ignore. She wasn't sure how she'd got herself into this. Liam had suggested she might like to go horse-riding with him. In a crazy moment she'd agreed, and now here she was, not at all sure she was ready for it. She'd last ridden a horse as a madcap teenager. The last thing she needed was to make a complete fool of herself and perhaps — horror of horrors — fall off! She couldn't bear it if she made a mess of it and Liam looked at her with contempt — or, even worse, with pity. Her hands were clammy as she gripped the steering wheel and turned the car in through the now-familiar gateway.

He was waiting for her, clad in beautifully cut formal riding clothes: tweed jacket over shirt and tie, close-fitting breeches and well-polished boots.

Jane glanced down in horror at her

old jeans and trainers. 'Liam,' she said shakily. 'You look very impressive. I'm sorry I can't match up.'

He took her hands and drew her close. 'This is an important moment for me, Jane. I wanted to do you justice. You're perfect, just as you are.' He held her to his heart. 'Hey, you're trembling. Not nervous, are you?'

'A little,' she mumbled into his chest. 'I don't want to let you down.'

'Now how could you do that?' He cupped her face in his hands and gently kissed her. 'It'll be fine, sweetheart, trust me.'

The horses were waiting, saddled and bridled. Liam helped her up onto a gentle little mare, then vaulted on to Sultan's back in the easy movement Jane had admired before, and the two of them moved off out of the yard and across the park.

Jane soon found she was enjoying herself. She adjusted to the horse's easy stride and realised that riding a horse was like riding a bike, or swimming.

Once learned, it was something you never forgot. The early morning air was crystal clear, the sun's rays just beginning to warm up, giving promise of a gorgeous summer's day to come.

Jane breathed in the heady, aromatic scent of wild thyme bruised underfoot as the horses' hooves brushed through the springy turf. Clouds of tiny blue butterflies danced among the flowers. Jane's heart soared. She realised that she hadn't acknowledged how much she'd missed this, and vowed to try and make horseriding a regular part of her life once again.

The trail led them up a steep track to a grassy knoll crowned with a clump of hawthorns. Liam halted his horse and turned to Jane. 'I wanted you to see this view,' he said. 'This is the perfect morning for it.'

She looked out over the countryside to a distant vista of blue sea bounded by white cliffs. A tiny ship sailed across the horizon, bound for France. The silence was broken only by a skylark rising up from the grass singing its matchless song, higher and higher into the sky until it was lost from sight.

Liam brushed Jane's thigh with his hand. His brooding eyes found hers, mirror to her own thoughts. Without speaking, he slipped from Sultan's back and held out his arms to her. He caught her as she slid down from the saddle and held her to him. She buried her face in his shoulder, breathing in the fresh, clean soap smell of his skin, mingled with the heathery aroma of his jacket. She could feel his heart beating in time with her own as she lifted her head and gazed into his eyes. 'Oh, Jane!' he murmured as his lips found hers. 'Jane, my beautiful girl.'

The two horses glanced at their riders, then dropped their heads and started grazing the sweet downland grass.

Liam spread his jacket on the damp grass, then pulled her down beside him on the soft springy turf. The sun glinted off the golden lights in her hair as they gazed, entranced, at the view, watching the little ship sail away out of sight. Jane sighed. It was a perfect morning, and yet there was still that niggling worry at the back of her mind.

He picked up on her mood. 'What is it, sweetheart? What's wrong?'

As clear as a bell, Jane heard again Lord Ashby's words of warning. *Watch your step. He has — unresolved issues.*

'Liam,' she said, unsure how to put it into words. 'Lord Ashby told me — he told me — there was something that happened before you came to Ashington. Something I needed to know, but he couldn't tell me.'

A shadow passed over Liam's face. His jaw tightened, a frown creased his brow. All at once he was the remote, lonely man she'd encountered on her first visit to the Estate. He stood up and walked a few paces away from her, striving to get his emotions under control. Then he turned to face her, his fists clenched.

'So the old man's been looking out

for you, has he?' His voice was bitter. 'I thought I'd left all that trouble behind me and it was dead and buried. But maybe his Lordship's right. If we are going to be as close as I'd like us to be, there can be no secrets. You deserve to make up your own mind.'

He turned away from her, and Jane could see by the tension in his shoulders just how deep his feelings went. He came and sat down beside her again, not looking at her, picking at the grass with restless fingers. 'It was when I was at the racing stable in Ireland. It was my first job and I was passionate about it. I'd grown up on the family farm, with my sister Maura and younger brother Declan. He was the apple of my dad's eye. He was the one who was going to take on the farm and make a success of it. As it happens, I didn't want to be a farmer. I was happy for Dec to have it. The only thing I cared about was riding and caring for horses, so I was made up when a local racing trainer took me on as a stable lad, doing all the usual jobs given to youngsters — mucking out the stables, cleaning endless saddles and bridles, sweeping the yard, even whitewashing the stones along the driveway. You know the sort of thing.'

Jane nodded, not wanting to interrupt.

'I worked hard, the boss was pleased with me and I gradually moved up the ladder, taking on some of the horses myself and riding out at exercise.'

'But you didn't become a jockey.'

'That's what I was aiming for. It was my dream. But the skinny little sixteen-year-old kid suddenly started to grow. After a couple of years, I ended up too tall.'

Jane could sense the disappointment was still there, just under the surface. 'So what did you do? Did they keep you on?'

'My boss was a fair man. I'll say that for him. He knew I was good with the horses and I found my place training the youngsters. I was all set to become a fully-fledged trainer in my own right.'

Jane couldn't quite see where the story was going, but kept quiet.

'Then something happened at home.' He paused, raking at the grass with his fingers, bouncing tiny white chalky pebbles in his palm. 'It was young Declan. He'd become a bit of a tearaway — because he was Mum's blue-eyed baby boy, he'd been spoilt and he thought he was above the law.

'Well, one night our paths crossed at the pub. I'd had my usual one Guinness. The boss was strict with all us lads and we knew our limitations.

Then Dec and a crowd of his mates came in. They'd been doing the round of bars in town and they were all roaring drunk, itching for trouble. When the landlord refused to serve them, I could see things were really going to kick off, so I hauled him outside and marched him to his car. Then he refused to give me the keys and insisted on driving himself. Well, it was only a couple of miles home and the roads were deserted so, fool that I was, I decided to risk it. I sat in the passenger seat and let him drive.'

He looked up at her, misery etched on his face. 'Jane, it was the biggest mistake of my life. There was an accident — inevitable, you'd think. Oh, no one was killed, that was a miracle, but he ploughed into a car parked on the side of the road. There was an explosion of some sort.'

'The petrol tank, probably,' Jane murmured, not wanting to interrupt.

'That's right. It set fire to the hedge, which destroyed a barn full of hay. It was a windy night, the fire spread to a derelict cottage and almost killed a young homeless man dossing down for the night — oh, it was terrible.'

'So what happened, Liam? I don't understand how it affected you so badly that you had to leave.'

He grunted in disgust. 'Dec was terrified at what he'd done, so on the spur of the moment I told the Garda I'd been driving. The car was awash with alcohol from the bottles stashed on the back seat, it was all over my clothes, and when I took the blame for him they believed me. I was in danger of losing my licence and being charged with dangerous driving. That would have meant the sack from my job as well, so before the case came to court, like an idiot I fled the country. My brother got off scot-free, and as far as I know he's never owned up to what really happened that night.

'I found a job with a racing stable in Yorkshire. I'd told my new employer the whole story, of course, thankfully he gave me the benefit of the doubt, and Lord Ashby was made aware of it when I moved down here to Dorset a few years later. But the charge still stands back home in Ireland, and if I ever set foot in the country again I run the risk of being arrested.'

Liam turned to face her. 'So that's my dark secret, sweetheart. I love my job here, and I'm damned lucky to have it, but I cut my ties with my family when I left. All except my sister. Maura still keeps in touch with me, but my parents took Declan's side and the rift between us is now so wide that I feel I won't ever be able to go back home.' The bitterness in his voice was heartbreaking. He added, 'I'm telling you this in confidence, Jane. Nobody knows about it here, other than Lord Ashby. That's how much I trust you.'

Jane was silent for a moment, taking in what he'd just told her. She took his hand and held it in both of her own.

'Liam,' she said. 'What you did was stupid, and you were the only one who got hurt. But you were trying to protect your brother, I can see that. I believe you, one hundred per cent. You've told me, that's enough for me, and it will never go any further, you have my word.'

He looked at her with a wry smile. 'You had to know, Jane, and if Lord Ashby hadn't prompted you to ask, I was going to get round to it, when the time was right. I've got too much to lose — you and Callum, as well as my job here at the estate. I know Lord Ashby trusts me, and I'll not easily betray that trust.' He jumped to his feet and pulled her up with him. 'Now let's get these horses back to the yard. And then I'm going to cook you breakfast!'

⋆　⋆　⋆

Liam's cottage was enchanting. Nestled in the trees, set in its own little garden, it was something straight out of a picture book. Jane exclaimed in delight as he opened the front door and ushered her in.

The entrance led straight into the living room, simply furnished with an old squashy sofa draped with a colourful throw, a small pine table with two high-backed wooden chairs tucked neatly underneath, a dresser holding an assortment of china plates and mugs. A log burner stood in the hearth, unlit today, and a massive oak beam above housed a collection of framed photo-graphs. Rustic-looking rag rugs warmed the stone flagged floor and there were chintz curtains at the two small windows. Jane could imagine how cosy it would be in winter, with the fire lit and the curtains drawn to keep out the cold. An open door led into a small kitchen. Jane could see a stove, a stone-ware sink and a shelf for pots and pans.

'Well?' asked Liam, 'What do you think? It's nothing fancy, but it comes with the job and it's all mine.'

'It's absolutely you, Liam.' Jane was charmed by the simplicity of the little cottage, neat as a new pin, everything in its place. He smiled his pleasure at her words.

'If you'd like to go and put the kettle on, I'll get out of this riding gear and change into something more comfort-able.' He laughed. 'But that's supposed to be your line, isn't it?' He disappeared through a door on the right hand side which Jane presumed led to the bedroom.

Jane gave into temptation and sneaked a look at the photographs on the mantelpiece. Liam with an older couple, obviously his parents. Liam as a young boy in school uniform. Liam with his arm round a young woman. Jane stood on tiptoe to get a clearer view, uncomfortably aware that she was being nosey.

'That's my sister, Maura.' Jane whirled round at his voice, guilt flaming her cheeks.

'I was just . . . ' Her voice tailed off. He was standing in the doorway, arms folded, clad only in his jeans, shirtless, regarding her with a quizzical smile playing round his lips. She gazed at him, taking in her first sight of his naked torso, marvelling at the powerful shoulders and broad chest, tapering to a perfect six-pack.

'Oh, Liam!' Sensible Jane fought a battle with her newly-awakened sensuous other self.

'It's time, sweetheart,' he whispered. It was a statement, not a question.

Dazed, she took his outstretched hand and he drew her gently towards the bedroom.

And then her mobile rang.

Liam groaned. 'Leave it,' he murmured imploringly. 'It's our time, Jane. We've earned it, surely.'

But the spell was broken.

9

The one person Jane could confide in was Vicky. She trusted the younger woman to give her sensible advice, and she knew her friend would never betray a confidence.

Vicky had picked up on Jane's agitated state as soon as she walked through the surgery door. 'What's up with you?' she asked. 'Is there something wrong with Callum? Or Cathy?'

Jane shook her head.

Vicky persisted. 'Don't tell me you fell off the horse!'

Jane managed a smile. 'Nothing like that. It's — it's Liam.'

Vicky narrowed her eyes, and waited.

'I can't go into it now, Vicks. It's too complicated.' She turned away, trying to get her brain into gear for the day's work. 'I'll tell you about it at coffee break.'

Vicky was seething with curiosity but had to keep her questions under wraps until morning surgery was through.

Plonking a mug of coffee down on the counter in front of Jane, she closed the door to the small kitchen. The last customer had finally left the surgery with medication for his puppy. The new assistant, Toby, had gone out on house calls.

'Now,' said Vicky firmly. 'Tell me what turned you into a seething mass of rampant hormones this morning.'

Jane, suddenly embarrassed, concentrated on stirring her coffee. 'Well, I told you I was going riding this morning. It was fine, I really enjoyed it. I'm thinking of taking it up on a regular basis, if Lord Ashby will let me borrow the horse.' She looked up at her friend, enthusiasm lighting up her eyes. 'It's been so long since I was on a horse, Vicky, and it was such an important part of my life when I was a kid, it's made me feel alive again.'

Vicky snorted derisively. 'And you

expect me to believe it was all about horses? Come off it, Jane, this is your Aunty Vicky you're trying to kid, not your mum.' Jane suddenly felt their roles had reversed, and that Vicky was the older, wiser one.

'No, it was afterwards. Liam invited me back to his cottage for breakfast.'

'That's a new angle.' Vicky snorted. Jane blushed scarlet.

'Well, he went to change, and then he appeared . . . '

'Come on, Jane, tell me. Confessions's good for the soul, you know.'

Jane, horribly tongue-tied, haltingly described what had happened, and how Liam had reacted when the call had interrupted them.

Vicky was her usual practical self. 'So how did *you* really feel when the phone rang? Were you devastated, or was a bit of you relieved to have a get-out? To be honest, I don't know what I would have done.'

Jane stirred her spoon round in her coffee, considering how to reply.

'I was going along with it, that's for sure, and if the interruption hadn't happened, then at that moment I would have been the happiest woman in the world.' She allowed herself a fleeting memory of Liam as she'd left him. 'He's so gorgeous, Vicky, sweet and gentle — no one could blame me.'

'Who said anything about blame? I'm not standing in judgement here,' Vicky protested. 'If he's what you want, and he makes you happy, then who am I to say you're wrong? But there's something about you, Jane, something that tells me it's not a hundred per cent right. So what is it?'

Jane stood up and moved restlessly round the room.

'If I knew that, I wouldn't have a problem. I guess I haven't, deep down, got used to the idea of someone else in my life other than Steve. He was my first love, and I suppose I thought he'd be my one and only. But after how he treated me, how can I trust another man not to treat me the same way?'

'But do you love Liam?' demanded Vicky, down to earth as usual.

'Yes,' said Jane quietly. 'That's part of the problem. I think I do. If it was just me, I'd not hesitate. Have a fling, enjoy it while it lasted. But there's still Callum. It always comes down to him. He really likes Liam, and I don't know if I can take the risk of letting him down again.'

Vicky had run out of ideas. She pushed back her chair and stood up.

'Well, I don't know what else to say to you, Jane. Maybe you should lighten up a bit, stop analysing everything and go with the flow. *Que sera, sera* — you know that old song? Whatever will be, will be. Just don't go doing anything silly, will you? Like cutting yourself off and living like a nun?'

Jane managed a shaky smile.

'I can't see that happening. I guess you're right. *Que sera, sera* it is — let's hope nobody gets hurt along the way.'

★ ★ ★

Cathy heard the rattle of the letterbox and just beat Honey to the front door to retrieve their copy of the local free newspaper. She spread it out on the table, expecting to see nothing more than the usual reports of the Parish Council, the activities of the Women's Institute and the cricket results.

Then she gasped. 'Jane! Come and have a look at this!'

The banner headline blazed up at them. LOCAL ESTATE MAN SOUGHT ON DRINK DRIVE CHARGE

'Oh *no!*' Jane muttered. 'How on earth did they get hold of that?'

'Look!' Cathy was reading the report. 'It's your friend Liam. Oh, I don't believe it. Jane, did you know about this?'

Before Jane could reply, her mobile's jingle announced the arrival of a text. With sinking heart Jane saw Liam's name on the screen.

I trusted you. How could you?

The brief message cut her to the quick. She grabbed her car keys and headed for the door. 'Got to go, Mum. I have to see him.' The door banged behind her as she whirled out and drove away, scattering gravel.

★   ★   ★

The stableyard was deserted. 'Liam!' she called, her voice echoing round the empty space. 'Liam! Lord Ashby! Anyone there?' In her desperation, she would almost have welcomed seeing Edmund or Fenella. They would have known where Liam was. But there was no answering voice.

She ran down the path that led to the cottage. She pushed at the half open door and stepped inside, suddenly afraid of what she would find. The little house felt abandoned, empty. His clothes had gone from the bedroom cupboard, the shelves tidy and his personal possessions missing.

'He's gone!' she whispered to herself. 'Liam, how could you believe that I'd betray you? You didn't even say goodbye.'

In a haze of misery, she found her way back to her car and slowly drove home. Cathy took one look at her distraught face and folded her daughter into her arms as if she'd been six years old.

'There, my, love,' she soothed. 'He'll turn up, I'm sure, when he's ready.'

But Liam didn't turn up. Nobody knew where he'd gone, there were no phone calls, no messages. Jane phoned and texted, but his phone was off.

'There's no more you can do, Jane,' sighed Cathy. 'If he really cares about you, he'll be in touch when he's ready.'

Jane knew she was right, but her usual common sense had deserted her. She was distraught.

'Liam, my darling, where are you?' she whispered to herself in bed at night, longing to feel his arms around her. She hugged her pillow to her, finding comfort in the bulk next to her body in the wakeful hours when her imagination ran riot. She pictured him lonely and alone, maybe living rough somewhere, staying out of sight, wondering if the police were looking for him. Now that he was gone, she realised just how much she loved and missed him. She wished with all her heart she'd stayed with him that last morning at the cottage. Now she might never get another chance to hold him, caress him, thrill to his touch.

She knew now — too late — that Liam was her soulmate and if — when — he came back, nothing and nobody on earth would keep them apart. She knew his secret now; knew that he'd done what he did for the sake of his family, and she knew now, finally, that nothing mattered but the man himself, and their love for each other.

10

A ring at the doorbell brought Callum running down the hallway. 'I'll get it, Mummy!' he called. But Cathy chased after him.

'Callum, come here! You know you're not allowed to answer the door in the evening.' She peered through the spyhole and gasped as she recognised the figure standing on the doorstep.

'Callum,' she hissed. 'Go and fetch Mummy, now!' The boy scooted down the hall to the kitchen, wondering who the mystery caller could be.

Cathy whipped off her pinny and stuffed it under her jacket draped over the end of the banisters. Glancing in the hall mirror she ran her hands through her hair and fiddled with the collar of her blouse. Then with what she hoped was a welcoming smile, she opened the door.

The elderly gentleman doffed his hat politely. 'Good evening, madam. You must be Jane's mother. I've heard a lot about you.'

'Lord Ashby,' stammered Cathy, wondering for a crazy moment if she ought to bob a curtsey. 'Do come in — I'll fetch Jane for you.'

She showed him into the immaculate sitting room, apologising for the non-existent mess. 'Do sit down. May I take your coat?'

Jane rescued her unusually flustered mother. 'How lovely to see you, Lord Ashby.' Hope sprang in her heart. 'Have you — have you any news?'

'I'll make coffee.' Cathy was glad to escape, to organise her thoughts.

Jane stood by the window, gazing out at the quiet darkening street, trying to take in what Lord Ashby had just told her. 'So you have heard from him! Is he all right? Where is he?'

Lord Ashby smiled sympathetically. 'Now then, Jane, not so fast. Yes, Liam did ring me, just a brief call, from a public phone, but I got the gist of what's happened.'

Jane crossed the room and sat beside the old man on the sofa.

'Please, you must tell me . . . '

He took her hands in hers. 'First of all, my dear, Liam is fit and well. He's gone to Ireland.'

'Ireland? But I thought he couldn't go back there.'

'That's the reason he's gone. As he said to me on the phone, he needs to clear up unfinished business before he can get on with his future. He's gone back to find out if he can fight the drink driving charge.'

'So what else did he say? Do you know any more?'

'I wish I did. His father has found him a good solicitor, and it seems hopeful his brother will have grown up enough to confess. He's got to sit it out and wait to see what they come up with. We'll just have to be patient, and wait for him to get in touch again.'

Jane stood up and paced the room,

unable to sit still. 'Did he say . . . anything else?'

'He asked how you were, of course, and just said to tell you he's sorry.' He paused, not wanting to cause the young woman more hurt. 'I'm sorry, Jane, but I don't think he will be coming back at any time soon.'

She moved slowly to the window, trying to hold back the tears. Her mother quietly brought in the steaming, fragrant coffee and left the room.

Lord Ashby cleared his throat, then went on, 'But there was another reason for my visit this evening. I discovered that it was my nephew, Edmund, who gave the story to the newspaper, and I've made sure that Liam knows the facts of that.'

Jane nodded. That made sense. Edmund was still out to cause mischief.

'I don't know how he found out about it, but it's been a wake-up call for all of us. I realise he's not had enough to do and I've told him he must change his ideas if he's to inherit the Estate.

I've threatened to leave it to the National Trust, or his cousin Fenella — which, in his eyes, would be worse!'

Not for the first time Jane wondered why, in this day and age, he was so insistent that the estate should go to a male heir, but it was not the time or place to ask.

'So what must he do to make you change your mind?'

'He's off to agricultural college, where he should have been straight after school. He needs to learn about estate management from the professionals. He has to realise he can't just drift into it, like some Victorian squire. I daresay he will find it hard to begin with, but he'll come away with, hopefully, a better sense of what his inheritance will bring: damned hard work, and mountains of paperwork.'

He was silent for a moment, reading Jane's thoughts. 'That means, of course you won't risk running into him when you come to see my horses.'

Jane felt a weight had lifted off her

shoulders. 'I must say that's a relief. I have to admit I was dreading coming face to face with him. And Fenella?'

The old man's face brightened. 'Ah now, I have hopes for that young lady. She's knuckled down and taken on some of the training of the show horses, in Liam's absence. She's becoming the granddaughter I always hoped she would be. It's taken this crisis to make her realise just how she was wasting her life. It may be early days, Jane, but I really think that with your shared interest in horses, you could be friends.

'Perhaps it was all my fault. I've been too lenient with the pair of them, trying to compensate them for the shortcomings of their parents.' He was silent for a moment, lost in thought. 'But I didn't come to talk about my family, Jane. No, I wanted to ask you a favour.'

'A favour? Me? What can I do?'

'Well now, it's about the County Show. I'm on the organising committee.'

Jane smiled. It was just the sort of

thing he would be involved with.

'You know, of course, that we have a team of vets on site for the whole three days of the show.' Jane nodded. It was something she'd wanted to do since she qualified, but she'd given up applying for the job. They always used the bigger, more prestigious vet practices — like Riverside.

Lord Ashby went on, 'One of our people has let us down and I am wondering if you could see your way to helping us out on one of the days?'

Jane's heart leapt. *Don't appear too keen*, she said to herself. *Play it cool.*

'It sounds interesting. It's the Bank Holiday weekend, of course. I'm not sure what we will be doing.' She couldn't keep it up. She smiled broadly and amazed Lord Ashby with a hug. 'I'd adore to do it! Of course I will.'

'Splendid! That's settled, then.' He glanced at his watch. 'I must be on my way. I've taken up enough of your evening.'

Jane found his coat and trilby hat and saw him to the door. 'Goodnight, Lord Ashby. Thank you for everything. And if you have any news of Liam . . .'

'I'll let you know, that's a promise. And you bring that boy of yours up to see us, hmmm? Make it soon, Jane. We miss having you around.'

Jane stood watching as he drove away, then closed the door and walked slowly back into the kitchen. Mixed emotions flooded through her. At least Liam was safe, although the likelihood of seeing him again was remote. But now there was the County Show to look forward to!

She suspected that Lord Ashby himself had played a large part in getting her the job. He made it sound as though she was doing him a favour, whereas in her opinion it was the other way round. The Show was intended to be a small consolation prize for the problems Edmund had caused.

She smiled ruefully to herself. It was

a kindly gesture but the loss of Liam was a terrible, piercing knife-wound. She wasn't sure how long it would take for her bruised and battered heart to heal.

11

Summer had arrived right on cue at the end of the school holidays. The County showground basked in unaccustomed sunshine, its sultry warmth tempered by a brisk breeze. Brightly coloured flags billowed and snapped bravely over the stalls and marquees, the displays of magnificent flora and fauna, perfect fruit and vegetables and demonstrations of country skills and crafts. The annual three-day show at the end of August was a magnet for families having a last day out before the serious business of back-to-school.

The welcome arrival of late summer sunshine enhanced the jolly holiday atmosphere as mums and dads, children and grandparents drifted from one gazebo-shaded stall to the next, picking up leaflets about anything from double glazing to swimming pools, sampling farmhouse cheese, fudge and home-made wine, or relaxing on the grass with their picnics and ice-creams. The events in the arena were under way, with a succession of pedigree animals being paraded before the judges.

Jane sat on the steps of the small caravan provided for the duty vets, enjoying the sights and sounds of the colourful kaleidoscope playing before her eyes. Cries of excited children, brass band music from somewhere out of sight, the crackly public address announcements, were all a familiar part of her summer scene. She'd been coming to the show since she was a small child, but now she was seeing it from an entirely different angle.

The duty vet, Jane discovered, had an early start, arriving at the showground as the sun came up over the trees. She'd checked in all the animals and found no problems.

She shaded her eyes against the sun's glare, searching for a glimpse of her family. Steve had been persuaded to bring Cathy and Callum along when it opened to visitors. She hoped, for Callum's sake, that his father might spend some time with him and not rush off to another important function. Country pursuits were not Steve's favourite thing, but there was plenty here to interest even him.

Jane spotted them at a stall selling leather jackets. Steve was deep in conversation with the Asian stallholder, haggling, Jane guessed, trying to get the price down. Callum was hanging about looking bored, kicking at the dust with his new trainers. Jane sighed. She should not have expected any more from her ex-husband. For all his fine talk on the joys of fatherhood, his own wishes would always come before those of his son. As she watched, Steve shook hands on the deal, and, his own interests catered for, wandered off with Callum in tow.

Her mug of coffee cooling beside her, Jane leaned back against the doorframe and closed her eyes, enjoying the peaceful moment. The sun shone on her upturned face and she gave herself up to its gentle caress.

It isn't fair, she thought. After the fiasco with Riverside's letter and Steve's admission of betrayal, she'd made a huge effort not to prejudice Callum against his father. Boys needed their dads, and Steve was the only adult male in his orbit at the moment. It was difficult for a boy growing up with his mother and grandmother.

If only Liam were here to share all this, she thought for the millionth time, *things could have been so different*. When she'd arrived at the showground she had not been able to help herself scanning the crowds for him, her heart skipping a beat every time she caught a glimpse of a tall, dark-haired man.

She knew she was being stupid, making herself miserable. Lord Ashby had heard nothing more from him since that brief phone call. Liam Delahaye had vanished from their lives as completely as if he'd never existed.

The strength of the wind had been increasing all day. The tall trees behind the horse lines bent to the rising force, sending restless flocks of rooks wheeling into the sky, and now turbulent banks of cloud built towers against the horizon, threatening a storm. Jane anxiously scanned the bronze-coloured sky, trying to judge whether the show was going to get through without a downpour. The last event was always the most popular: the parade of heavy horses. The magnificent shires and their immaculate wagons were timed to be the last to appear in the arena, to ensure the audience stayed until the end.

The spectators crowded the ringside, pressed against the ropes, as the horses entered the ring. Jane, standing on the caravan steps for a better view, caught her breath. The massive animals, so gentle and biddable in spite of their immense strength, always brought a lump to her throat. It was a picture of

Olde England, a cavalcade of rippling muscles, buffed and burnished to immaculate perfection; shining harness jingling with gleaming horse brasses, plumes and ribbons woven into manes and tails. The heavy wagons behind them, resplendent in their trade livery, were driven by bowler hatted grooms in buff coloured coats and shiny black boots.

Jane gazed, entranced, as the horses progressed around the arena to stately music. She imagined herself back in time to the age when horse power kept the wheels of industry and agriculture turning. Once threatened with extinction when their usefulness was eclipsed by steam and oil power, these magnificent beasts were now a cherished part of England's heritage.

Jane could see Callum, gazing open-mouthed at the enormous animals. Steve was a few yards behind him, talking on his mobile phone. There were still deals to be done, even on a Bank Holiday. He wasn't watching the arena. The only horses he was interested in were those which might win him a few pounds on the race course.

Jane looked anxiously at the sky as the clouds blocked out the sun and the wind gusted more strongly. A rumble of thunder growled in the distance. The guy ropes holding the tents and gazebos struggled to take the strain. Stallholders started packing up as anything not securely fixed down flew into the air. Discarded paper and picnic debris bowled along the grass.

The crowds were thinning as a steady stream of visitors snaked towards the exit. Callum was left standing alone by the ropes, still enraptured by the spectacle in the arena.

As the tempo of the music changed, the horses broke into a ponderous trot. A sudden crack of thunder with a blinding flash of lightning heralded the approaching storm. A violent surge of wind swept across the showground, snatching a white canvas sheet from its hoarding and sending it flapping and billowing towards the horses. It was too much for even these docile beasts. One reared up, dislodging its driver, and galloped, in panic, full-tilt towards the barrier. Towards Callum.

Jane watched in frozen horror as the scene unfolded in slow motion. She could hear someone screaming, then realised it was herself. Steve stood rooted to the spot, unable to move as the out-of-control horse and its heavy wagon bore down on his son.

At the last moment a man raced out from the crowd and threw himself on top of the boy, knocking him to the ground, receiving a glancing blow on the head from one of the iron-clad hooves, as big as dinner plates, and taking on his own body the weight of the heavy wooden wheels of the cart. There was a heartbeat of absolute silence and stillness before all hell let loose: spectators dashing in all directions to get away from the horse, screaming, crying, the public address announcer vainly appealing for calm.

In the midst of the pandemonium, the body of the stranger who had shielded her son lay motionless on the ground. As Jane watched, unable to even think about what might have happened to Callum, a small trainer-clad foot appeared from underneath the man's thigh. Then, amazed, she saw her boy struggle out and stagger to his feet. As Jane rushed over and folded him in her arms, he started to cry.

The St John Ambulance team were working on the ominously still body of the man lying broken in the dust, trying to assess his injuries, focused on their task. The woman officer who seemed to be in charge sat back on her heels. 'I've got a pulse. Where's that ambulance got to? Tell them to hurry.'

Jane was desperate to find out how badly hurt her Good Samaritan was, but she knew she could help best by keeping out of the way. He was alive; that was all she knew.

Steve, shocked at last into action, came across and tried to comfort

Callum. Jane looked at him with contempt. 'You were supposed to be looking after him,' she said coldly. 'You just stood there and let a complete stranger risk his life to save him. What sort of a father does that make you?'

Then, utterly drained, she whispered, 'Just go, Steve. Leave us alone.'

Jane crouched beside Callum, holding him close, shielding him from the scene behind them as the paramedics gently turned the injured man on to his back and lifted him on to a stretcher. She didn't want Callum to see anything which might traumatise him even more. He wriggled and peered over her shoulder. 'Look, Mummy!'

'Don't, darling. The man's very poorly. You don't want to see.'

Callum insisted. 'No, Mummy, look! It's Mr Holiday.'

As Jane, gripped by a sudden chill, slowly turned her head in disbelief, the first fat drops of rain began to fall.

★   ★   ★

Jane remembered little of the nightmare journey to hospital in the ambulance. The torrential rain had brought a sudden end to the Bank Holiday. The roads were awash with rainwater and choked with cars and it seemed to Jane that their progress was painfully slow, despite the flashing blue light and ear-splitting siren.

The joy she should have felt at Liam's return was eclipsed by the agonising knowledge that he was seriously hurt. The paramedic riding with them could tell her little, other than that the casualty was stable and comfortable. He glanced at Jane, concerned, and draped a blanket round her shoulders, recognising signs of shock. He patted her hand.

'We'll do our best for him, love. He's a strong young chap, by the looks of him. Just hang on in there. He'll need you.'

Liam was deeply unconscious, his face deathly pale, almost invisible under the oxygen mask. Her eyes devoured him, hungry for the sight of him, trying to memorise every little detail. She reached out and touched his hand. It was cold — so cold she felt like crying. She wrapped her hands around his, trying to warm him, remembering the way those long strong fingers had caressed her, gently coaxing, waiting patiently for her to trust him.

'Liam,' she whispered, although she knew he couldn't hear. 'You must live, my darling. Live, for me — for us. You came back and saved the life of my boy. Don't leave us again, Liam. We need you. Stay and let me love you, Liam, stay for me and for Callum.' She whispered the words over and over, like a mantra: 'Stay, Liam. Stay for me and for Callum. Stay . . . '

12

The small room was warm and peaceful, only the reassuring background hum and occasional bleep from the monitors recording the progress of Liam's fight for life disturbing the quiet. He was lying propped on the bed, unrecognisable beneath the forest of tubes, drips and wires attached to every visible inch of his body. His head was swathed in bandages.

Jane was slumped in a chair beside the bed, her head supported on her hand, dozing. She'd tried to stay awake but exhaustion had finally wafted her into fitful sleep, disturbed by fearful dreams of giant horses trampling over everything and everyone she loved.

As a nurse entered the room, she was instantly awake, glad to be dragged from her nightmare.

'Sorry, dear, I tried to be quiet. You

must be worn out.' The woman in her trim uniform smiled sympathetically.

Jane yawned, stretched, and rubbed sleep from her eyes. 'How is he? Is there any change?' she asked anxiously.

She'd been told very little the evening before, when they'd arrived in the ambulance. The medical team had swarmed around Liam's unconscious body, intent on their vital tasks. Jane had volunteered what little information she knew about him: his name and his employer, but she'd had to admit she didn't know his date of birth or how to contact his next of kin, only that they were somewhere in Ireland. 'I'm a friend,' she'd told them. 'Just a friend, but at the moment I'm all he's got.'

She had sat in the waiting area, trying to remain calm, but eaten up with terror that she might lose him at the very moment he'd come back to her. The cavalcade of doctors and nurses with Liam at its centre disappeared through double doors to the treatment area. There was nothing she could do except wait. And hope.

After a long wait, a consultant had told her that Liam had a serious head injury, several broken ribs and severe internal bruising, but nothing needing surgery. 'It's the head injury we're most concerned about,' he'd told her. 'That, and the damage to his spine. We don't know at this stage how long-lasting that will be.'

He'd looked with sympathy at the young woman's stricken face, wishing he could tell her something more positive. 'I'm sorry,' he said gently, 'but it's a question of wait and see at this stage. But he's a strong, healthy man. That's all I can say at the moment.'

The nurse checked the monitors, recorded Liam's temperature and pulse on a chart clipped to the foot of the bed, and smoothed the sheets.

'There's no change,' she said to Jane. 'He's stable, his heart is strong. That's a good sign.' She moved quietly round the room, efficient, confident. 'Why don't you go for a cup of tea? I'll stay with him until you get back.'

Jane realised that maybe the nurse needed her out of the way whilst she attended to her patient. She stood up, stretching the cramp out of her legs, and set off to find her way to the hospital canteen. Tea and toast suddenly seemed very inviting.

The hospital, built on a large out-of-town site, had beautifully landscaped gardens. Jane found a bench in a peaceful, sunny spot beside the lake and pulled out her phone. Cathy answered at the first ring.

'Jane! Thank goodness. I've been going out of my mind with worry. How is he? Have they told you anything? Is there anything I can do?'

Jane broke in, protesting. 'Mum, slow down, let me get a word in. Liam's in a bad way but they say he's as well as can be expected. Whatever that means. They can't tell me anything until he wakes up.' She paused for a moment. The little maverick word 'if' slid into her mind. She determinedly pushed it away. 'Now, how is Callum? I feel awful about leaving him, but Liam's got no-one else.'

'Hello, Mummy.' Callum butted in. 'Can I come and see Mister Holiday? Is he going to be better soon?'

'Callum darling, he's still quite poorly. You can't come just yet, but as soon as the doctor says it's okay, Grandma will bring you.'

Jane wasn't sure how much to tell him. She didn't want to sound too gloomy, but she needed to be realistic about Liam's chances. 'Why don't you make Mr Holiday a get well card?' she suggested. 'That will be sure to cheer him up. I expect he's been missing you too, you know.'

'Okay, Mummy. I'll do a picture of Jigsaw, shall I?'

Jane smiled to herself. Callum was no artist, but it would give him something to work at, and Cathy would lend a hand.

'That sounds wonderful. Just the thing to make him feel better. Now,

Callum, I'm not sure when I'll be able to come home, so be a very good boy for Grandma.' She paused, a lump in her throat. 'I love you, Callum.'

'Love you too, Mummy.'

And I love Liam, she added silently, *more than I ever thought possible.*

Returning to the room on the ward where the still, silent figure lay on the bed, she stroked his hand, willing him to move just the tip of one finger. The monitors hummed and bleeped, and Liam remained deeply unconscious, unaware of the fight for his life going on around him.

★　★　★

By the end of the third day, Jane was exhausted. Cathy had brought in fresh clothes for her and tried to persuade her to come home. Jane refused.

'They say he could wake at any time, and I must be here for him.'

'I do see, that, love, but honestly, you won't do him any favours by making yourself ill. Callum needs you, and goodness knows how Toby and Vicky are managing to keep the business going.'

'I'm sorry, Mum, but Callum's got you, the business can look after itself for a week or two, but Liam's only got me.' She paused. 'The consultant told me to talk to him. He said nobody knows how much he might be able to hear. So if I keep letting him know I'm here, it might bring him back sooner.'

Cathy knew when she was beaten. 'Just don't wear yourself out. You'll need to get some rest. When he does come round, you won't want to be too exhausted to help him. Just think about it, Jane.'

'I'll be fine, Mum. You know me — I can catnap anytime. Now off you go and give Callum the biggest hug from me.'

★　★　★

Jane woke with a start, in the half-light of early morning, stiff and chilly in her chair. She listened, wondering whether some sound from outside had disturbed her, but she could hear nothing. Her gaze turned to Liam, lying still and remote as a statue.

'Hello, Liam,' she began. 'It's me again. I'm sorry if you can hear me and all this aimless chatter is driving you crazy. I'll stop — just as soon as you give me the word.'

She stared at his face, longing for a sign that he was in there. Then she saw his eyelids flicker. She caught her breath. Had she imagined it?

'Liam!' she whispered. 'Liam, my darling, I'm here for you.'

His face twitched, he drew in a long breath, then slowly his eyes opened. He turned his head and gazed at her.

'Jane,' he croaked. 'So I finally got you to stay the night with me.'

Jane knew she should call the nurse, but she craved a few moments alone with him. She kissed him gently, the stubble of four days' growth against her face. She traced the line of his cheek with her finger and the outline of his mouth. She gazed into his dark eyes, drinking in the reality of him, knowing that her place was by his side, in sickness or in health.

'Liam,' she whispered again. 'You've come back to me.' She eased on to the bed and stretched out beside him, her heart full of love and hope.

When the nurse came in a little while later, she found Liam awake, smiling, and clasping the hand of the woman fast asleep beside him.

★ ★ ★

The consultant was furious. 'I hope you realise, Mrs Pardoe,' he said icily, 'that you might have done untold damage. Your action was reckless and irresponsible. I would have thought you'd have had more sense.'

Jane stared at the floor, her cheeks burning with embarrassment. She'd only meant to have a few private minutes with Liam before the medics took over. If she'd caused him more harm, she'd never forgive herself.

The consultant spoke to Liam. 'Mr Delahaye, you have several broken ribs, which will heal in time. You fortunately did not suffer any damage to your skull other than the laceration, which has been stitched. It's the bruising to your spine which is causing us most concern. Can you move your toes?'

'No,' answered Liam. 'I can't.'

The day which had started so well turned into a nightmare. Liam was paralysed from the waist down. All the specialists agreed that there was no permanent damage to his spine and in time he should regain the feeling in his legs and be able to walk, but Jane knew the battle was only beginning.

Cathy brought Callum in to visit. The small boy gazed in awe at Liam's bandages and all the equipment ranged round the bed. Suddenly shy, he hid his head in his mother's lap.

'Come along, sweetheart,' she encouraged him, shaking his shoulder. 'What are you going to say?'

Brave again, Callum took a deep breath and piped up, 'Thank you for saving me, Mr Holiday.'

Liam took the home-made card from him and regarded it gravely. 'Now isn't that the best picture I've ever seen? That's Jigsaw there — that's just altogether grand, so it is. Who helped you draw the horse, Callum? You must have had some help.'

Callum, now grinning from ear to ear, shook his head.

'I did it all by myself, of course. And I did the writing.'

Get Well, it said in shaky multi-coloured capital letters on the front of the card, and *Love from Callum* inside.

'Did you now?' He ruffled the boy's hair and they exchanged a grin.

⋆ ⋆ ⋆

The euphoria Jane had felt when Liam regained consciousness receded as day followed day without any visible sign of progress. Lord Ashby had paid for him

188

to be transferred to a private clinic where he had a ground floor room opening on to a sheltered terrace, and an en-suite bathroom. Jane still came to visit him every day, and when the weather was fine, pushed him outside in a wheelchair. She knew he found his disability hard to accept. He grew morose and withdrawn, and then he dropped his bombshell.

'It's been grand having you around, Jane, so it has. But I've got work to do now if I'm going to get better, and it will be easier if I know you're getting on with your life.'

She was shocked to the core. This was the last thing she expected.

'But — Liam! I want to be with you. I so nearly lost you — what would I do without you?'

'Your family needs you more than I do just now. I don't want you visiting. You're too much of a reminder of what we might have had. For now, you have to leave me to work things out for myself.'

'Don't you love me any more, Liam? Is that what you're saying?'

'Of course I love you, my darling, More than life itself. But like this I'm no use to you. Without my legs, I've got no future — as a man or as a lover. I want you with me, Jane — you know that. I always have. But not as my nurse or my mother, pushing me around in a chair, helpless as a baby. Forget about me. Go and find yourself a real man.'

He turned his face away from her, his jaw set, his eyes stony. Inside, his heart was breaking as he watched her walk away.

* * *

Jane was in despair. She could not have foreseen that he would reject her. She opened her heart to Vicky. 'Where did I go wrong, Vicks?' she sobbed. 'After everything that's happened, he's pushed me away. I only wanted to look after him.'

'That's the problem, isn't it? He's a

proud man. He knows he can't manage on his own right now, but he doesn't want to be dependent on the woman he loves. You'll have to respect his wishes, Jane. If you try to interfere, you could make matters worse.'

Jane got up from the table, took their coffee mugs to the sink and ran the tap. She'd thought she was unhappy before, when he vanished from her life, but now, knowing that Liam was just a few miles away, it was torture. She'd imagined that they would be able to pick up the pieces of their relationship and life would be wonderful.

She had a nagging feeling that somehow it was her fault. 'I should never have turned him down,' she lamented to Vicky. 'If we'd been a proper couple, Edmund would have accepted it and not tried to make trouble for him . . . Liam wouldn't have gone away . . . oh, Vicky, it's all my fault. It's such a mess.' She wiped her eyes and blew her nose. Vicky hugged her.

'You were trying to do the best for everybody. And Liam wouldn't have respected you if you'd been too eager, would he?'

Jane managed a shaky smile. 'You're probably right. But now — it looks like I'll never get the chance.'

★   ★   ★

The summer had slipped past. The leaves on the trees were turning gold and orange and brown. The days grew shorter, and autumn, melancholy with regret for the season's passing, was upon them.

Jane had kept her promise. She'd stayed away from Liam, respecting his decision, but she mourned the loss of the lover she might have had.

Then, when she was beginning to give up hope of ever seeing him again, she had a call from the clinic director. 'Mrs Pardoe? Mr Delahaye is asking for you.' Jane's heart thumped in her chest.

'Is he — is he worse?' she stammered. 'Why now?'

'Just come, Mrs Pardoe. As soon as you like.'

Shakily Jane walked up to the reception desk. 'I've come to see Mr Delahaye,' she announced. 'Is he still in the same room?'

The receptionist, immaculate in her white tailored overall, smiled at her.

'He is — go on down, you know the way.'

Her heart pounding, Jane found her way along the corridor. Liam's door was half open. She tapped gently and pushed, afraid of what she might find.

He was sitting in his chair by the window.

'Liam,' she said unsteadily, suddenly shy. 'You asked to see me. Is there something wrong?'

He turned slowly to face her. 'Jane,' he said quietly. He held out his hands to her. She crossed the room, knelt by the chair, took his face in her hands and gazed into his eyes.

'What's wrong? Why ask me to come now, after all this time?'

He laughed softly and, planting his feet firmly on the floor, rose to his feet, pulling her up with him. Jane gasped, lost for words.

'This, sweetheart, is what I've got to tell you.' He folded his arms around her, held her tight against his heart. 'Ah, Jane, it's been a long haul. But I'm whole again, my love, I can be the man you want me to be.'

She gazed into his eyes, not fully believing what she was hearing.

He dropped his head to hers and slowly, tenderly, began to claim her mouth in a gentle kiss. She pushed him away, suddenly angry.

'So, Liam, after all this time, with no word from you, weeks when I've not been allowed to see you — suddenly everything's all right, is it? I've had to try and get on with my life, in limbo, waiting to hear from you.'

She turned away. 'You decide you're well again, snap your fingers and expect me to come running? You told me to find myself a 'proper man' as you charmingly put it. How do you know I've not taken you at your word?'

He looked shocked. 'I — I'm sorry, Jane, I'm taking you for granted. It's just that I've wanted you so much, worked so hard for this moment. I didn't consider your feelings at all.' He looked broken, turned away, his fists clenched. 'If there's someone else, tell me now, Jane, and I'll stay out of your life.' His voice ended on a sob that broke Jane's heart.

She put her arms round him, turned him to face her, her anger gone.

'No, Liam,' she said gently. 'There's no one else. Only you. You're the man I want, for me and my son.' She ran her hands over his shoulders, feeling his muscles relax as she moved closer.

'Hold me,' she whispered. 'All that time without you, you can't know what it's been like.'

He smiled into her eyes. 'Oh yes, sweetheart, I know exactly what it was like.' He tightened his arms, holding her against him as she lifted her face to his kiss, as they silently pledged themselves one to the other.

At length she stirred in his arms and pulled away.

'Liam,' she murmured. 'Let's go home.'

THE END

We do hope that you have enjoyed reading this large print book.

Did you know that all of our titles are available for purchase?

We publish a wide range of high quality large print books including:
Romances, Mysteries, Classics
General Fiction
Non Fiction and Westerns

Special interest titles available in large print are:
The Little Oxford Dictionary
Music Book, Song Book
Hymn Book, Service Book

Also available from us courtesy of Oxford University Press:
Young Readers' Dictionary
(large print edition)
Young Readers' Thesaurus
(large print edition)

For further information or a free brochure, please contact us at:
Ulverscroft Large Print Books Ltd.,
The Green, Bradgate Road, Anstey,
Leicester, LE7 7FU, England.
Tel: (00 44) **0116 236 4325**
Fax: (00 44) **0116 234 0205**

SECRETS IN THE SAND

Jane Retallick

When Sarah Daniels moves to a sleepy Cornish village her neighbour, local handyman and champion surfer, Ben Trelawny is intrigued. He falls in love with her stunning looks and quirky ways — but who is this woman? Why does she lock herself in her cottage — and why she is so guarded? When Ben finally gets past Sarah's barriers, a national newspaper reporter arrives in the village. Sarah disappears, making a decision that puts her life and future in jeopardy.

WITHOUT A SHADOW OF DOUBT

Teresa Ashby

Margaret Harris's boss, Jack Stanton, disappears in suspicious circumstances. The police want to track him down, but Margaret believes in him and wants to help him prove his innocence. Meanwhile, Bill Colbourne wants to marry her, but, unsure of her feelings, she can't think of the future until she finds Jack. And, when she does meet with him in Spain, she finally has to admit to Bill that she can't marry him — it's Jack Stanton who she loves.

LOVE OR NOTHING

Jasmina Svenne

It seemed too good an opportunity to miss . . . Impoverished by her father's death, Kate Spenser has been forced to give up music lessons, despite her talent. So when the enigmatic pianist John Hawksley comes to stay with her wealthy neighbours, Kate cannot resist asking him to teach her. She was not to know Hawksley's abrupt manner would cause friction between them, nor that the manipulative Euphemia would set out to ensnare the one man who seemed resistant to her charms . . .

AN IMITATION OF LOVE

Sally Quilford

Catherine Willoughby's brother, Jimmy, has been providing forged documents to help the mysterious 'Captain' assist prisoners escaping from Revolutionary France. When Jimmy is murdered, Catherine and her sister, Alyssa, become wards of Xander Oakley, a dandy whom Catherine despises. Both Catherine and Xander have their secrets, including the love they're beginning to feel for each other. When Catherin runs away, she heads straight into danger. Can Xander save her before it's too late to reveal what's in his heart?